JUNGLE TALES

First published 1913
This edition published by Lector House in 2024

ISBN: 978-93-6138-592-6

Lector House LLP
Registered Office: H. No. 96, Block C, Tomar Colony,
Burari, Delhi – 110084, India
info@lectorhouse.com
www.lectorhouse.com

JUNGLE TALES

BITHIA MARY CROKER

2024

LECTOR HOUSE LLP

HER BLACK EYES BLAZED WITH EXCITEMENT.

JUNGLE TALES

BY

B. M. CROKER

Author of
'Pretty Miss Neville,' 'Diana Barrington,'
'The Spanish Necklace,'
'In Old Madras,' etc.

A NEW IMPRESSION
WITH A FRONTISPIECE BY JOHN CHARLTON

"Ah! what a warning for thoughtless man,
Could field or grove, could any spot of earth,
Show to his eye an image of the pangs
Which it hath witnessed!"

Wordsworth.

THESE TALES ARE INSCRIBED
TO
OLD FRIENDS
IN THE CENTRAL AND NORTH-WEST PROVINCES
IN MEMORY OF
MANY PLEASANT HOURS IN CAMP AND CANTONMENT.

B. M. C.

Contents

VILLAGE TALES
AND
JUNGLE TRAGEDIES.

A Free-Will Offering.

"Kismiss," as the natives call it, is anything but a jovial and merry season to me, and I heartily sympathize with those prudent souls who flee from the station or cantonment, and bury themselves afar off in the jungle, until the festive season has been succeeded by the practical New Year! Christmas in India is an expensive anniversary to a needy subaltern such as I am. Putting aside the necessary tips to the mess-servants, the letter-corporal, and colour-sergeant, I have my own retinue (about ten in number), who overwhelm me with wreaths and flowers culled from my garden, and who expect, in return, solid rupees of the realm. This is reasonable enough; but it passes the limits of reason and patience when other peopled body-servants, peons, syces, and all the barrack dhobies, and every "dog" boy in the station, lie in ambush in order to thrust evil-smelling marigolds under my nose, with expectant salaams! Last Christmas cost me nearly the price of a pony—this Christmas, I resolved to fly betimes with my house-mate, Jones of the D.P.W. We would put in for a week's leave, and eat our plum-pudding at least sixty miles from Kori.

Alas! my thrifty little scheme was knocked on the head by a letter from my cousin Algy Langley. He is the eldest son of an eldest son; I am the younger son of a second son: and whereas I am a sub. in an infantry regiment, grilling on the plains of India, and working for my daily bread, Algy has run out for one cold weather, merely in search of variety and amusement.

"Why on earth should relations think it necessary to meet on one particular day, in order to eat a tasteless bird and an indigestible pudding?"

I put this question to Jones, as we sat in our mutual verandah, opening the midday dâk.

"Just look at this; it's a beastly nuisance!" and I handed him Algy's note, which said—

> "Dear old Perky (my Christian name is Perkin),—This is to give notice that I am coming to eat my Christmas dinner with you. I arrive on the 21st, per mail train.—Yours, "A. Langley."

"What is your cousin like?" inquired Jones.

"Oh, a regular young London swell, who has never roughed it in his life. I suppose I shall have to turn out of my room," I grumbled; "and I must borrow Robinson's bamboo cart to meet him, for I believe he would faint if I put him in a bullock tonga at first—he must arrive at that by degrees!"

"Is there no chance of our getting off to Karwassa? Wouldn't he come and have a try for the man-eater?" urged Jones.

"Not he!" I rejoined emphatically; "he is a lady-killer—that is his only kind of sport. I'm glad I have not put in for my leave; you and I will go later—the tiger will wait."

"Yes, he has waited a good while," retorted Jones, sarcastically; "nearly three years, and about a dozen shikar parties have been got up for his destruction, and still he keeps his skin! But, somehow, I have a presentiment that *we* shall get him."

* * * * *

The next day Jones and I met Algy at the station. He had brought three servants, a pile of luggage, and looked quite beautiful as he stepped out on the platform, wearing a creaseless suit, Russia-leather boots, gloves, and a white gauze veil to keep off the dust. His handkerchief was suggestive of the most "up-to-date" delicate scent, as he passed it languidly over his forehead, and gave directions to have his late compartment cleared.

As books, an ice-box, fruit, a fan, cushions, and a banjo, were handed out one by one, I gathered, from Jones's expressive glance, that he granted that my cousin was a hopeless subject for the jungle.

"Well, Perky," he said, slapping me on the back, "I've got everything now—what are you waiting for?"

"Your lady's-maid," I promptly answered, as I nodded at the banjo, pillows, and fan.

"I like to be comfortable," he confessed. "One may as well take one's ease as not; it has an excellent and soothing effect on the temper."

But I noticed that he caught sight of Jones's grin, and coloured deeply—whether with rage or shame, I could not guess. As I drove my guest up to our lines, I secretly marvelled as to what had brought him to our little Mofussil station, a two days' railway journey through the flattest, ugliest country. He had been staying at Government House, Calcutta, at various splendid Residencies, and had had every opportunity of seeing India from the most commanding and luxurious point of view. Why had he sought *me* out?

Later on, as we sprawled in long chairs in my portico overlooking a sun-baked compound,—with a view chiefly consisting of the back of my neighbour's stables, and Jones's little brown bear, mowing and moping, under a scraggy mango tree,—I put the inevitable question:

"Well, Algy, what do you think of India?"

"Not much," he answered. "It is not a bit like what I have expected: it is not as Eastern as Egypt. The scenery that I have seen consists of bushes, boulders, and terra-cotta plains. I don't care about ruins and buildings; what I want to come at are the people and customs of the land—so far, it's all England, not India: England at the sea-side, dressing, dancing, racing, flirting; clothes are thinner, manners are easier; but it's England—England—England!"

I did what I could for him. I took him to a garden-party, to call on the beauty of the station, to write his name in the general's book, to mess, to a soldier's sing-song; and still he was discontented. He had been faintly amused with our "pot" gardens and trotting bullocks; nevertheless, he continued to grumble in this style—

"Your band plays the last new coster song, your ladies believe that they wear the latest fashions, your men read the latest news not two days old, your servants speak English and speak it fluently. Your butler plays the fiddle, and he told me this morning that my banjo was 'awfully nice.' I desire that you will introduce me (if you can) to India without European clothes—stripped and naked. I want to get below the surface, below officialdom, and general orders, and precedence; scrape the skin, and show me Hindostan."

"Show me something out of the common." This was his querulous parrot-cry.

"Would you care to come out into the jungle sixty miles away," I ventured, "to a place that has no English attributes, and help to shoot a notorious man-eating tiger? There is a reward of five hundred rupees for his skin. For the last two years he has devastated the country."

"Like it!" cried Algy, suddenly, sitting erect, "why, it's the very thing. I'll go like a shot. I am ready to start to-night. What's the name of the place?"

"Karwassa. This man-eater has killed, they say, more than a hundred people, and if we shoot him, we cover ourselves with glory; if we fail, we are no worse than half the regiment, and most of the station."

Algy figuratively leapt at the idea; he was out of his chair, pacing the verandah, long ere I had ceased to speak.

"How soon could we start?"

"As soon as I obtained leave," I replied.

"Oh, bother leave!" he retorted, impatiently.

"Still, it is a necessary precaution," I answered. "If I go without it I shall be cashiered, and *that* would be a bother."

"All right; put in for it at once. The sooner we are off the better," cried Algy. "Let us get the first shikari in the province, and if he puts us fairly on the tiger, the five hundred rupees shall be his. I pay all expenses."

"But Jones wants— —"

"Yes, Jones, by all means," he interrupted; "you had better lay your heads together without delay. He told me he was a born organizer, so you might, perhaps, leave the transport and commissariat in his hands, whilst you secure leave, and the keenest and best shikari. Money *no* object."

"You are keen enough, Algy," I remarked; "but, of course, you have no experience of big game. *Can* you shoot?"

"I can hit a stag, and I've accounted for crocodile, but I have never seen a tiger in a wild state."

"Ah! and you'll find a tiger is quite another pair of shoes," I assured him impressively.

The day before Christmas we started in the highest spirits. Algy wore a serviceable shikar suit, strong blue putties, and shooting-boots, and looked as workmanlike as possible. Our destination, Karwassa, lay sixty miles due north, and we travelled forty-five miles along the smooth trunk road in a dogcart, with relays of horses, and arrived early in the afternoon at Munser Dâk Bungalow—a neat white building, in a neat little compound, that was almost swallowed up by the surrounding jungle. Here we experienced our first breakdown. Jones prided himself on doing everything on a "system"—but the system failed ignominiously. Our luggage and servants were fifteen miles behind, and we could not proceed that night, so we resigned ourselves into the hands of the Dâk bungalow khansamah, who slew the usual Dâk bungalow dinner for our behoof. There was a fair going on in the village, and we strolled across to inspect it. A fair of the kind was no novelty to me; but Algy was childishly delighted with all he witnessed, and stood gazing in profound amazement at the stalls of Huka heads, pewter anklets, bangles, and coarse, bright native cloths for turbans and sarees; the money was chiefly copper pice and cowrie shells—the shell currency was a complete revelation to our Londoner, as was a tangle-haired, ash-bedaubed fakir, with his head thrust through a square iron frame, so devised that rest was impossible. He could never lean back, never lie down, never know ease. He had worn this instrument of torture for twelve years, and was a most holy man—so Nuddoo, the shikari, informed us.

"But what is the good of it?" demanded Algy. "What the dickens does he do it for?"

"For a vow," was the solemn reply.

"I'd rather be dead than have to wear an iron gate round my neck," rejoined Algy. "But I suppose he thinks he is doing the right thing, and probably he is a good sort."

And he gave the good sort five rupees.

Next morning we started in real earnest, for the real jungle—each on a separate little cart or chukrun, drawn by a pair of small trotting bullocks; the driver rode on the pole, and behind him there was just room for one person, if he curled himself up, and sat cross-legged. We formed quite a long procession, as we passed down the village street, and all the population came out to speed the sahibs, "who were going to try and shoot the Karwassa man-eater." Judging by their looks, they were by no means sanguine of our success.

Our road was a mere track, up and down the sides of shallow water-courses, across the dry beds of great rivers, over low hills, and through heavy jungle. The country grew wilder and wilder; here and there we scared a jackal, here and there a herd of deer; villages were very few and far between, and we had passed two that were absolutely deserted: melancholy hamlets, with broken chatties, abandoned ploughs, and grass-grown hearths—now the abode of wild dogs. We were gradually approaching our destination, a cattle country, below a long range of densely wooded hills; having halted at midday to rest our animals for a few hours, we then set out again. But twenty miles is a long distance for a little trotting bullock, especially if his head be turned from home. The eager canter, or brisk trot, had now become a mere spasmodic crawl; for the last mile Algy—the most keen and energetic of the party—had been belabouring and shouting at his pair. What a sight for his club friends, could they have beheld him, the elegant Algy, hoarse, coatless, and breathless! In spite of his desperate exertions, his cattle came to a full stop, and suddenly lay down—an example promptly followed by others. "Darkness was coming," urged Nuddoo, pointing to the yellow sunset. "We were near an evil country, and it was about *his* usual time. Karwassa was two koss further, and we had best camp and light fires, and spend the night where we had halted. The sahibs could sleep under the carts, their servants were in waiting, also their food—all would be well."

I must honestly confess that I thought this a most sensible proposition; but Algy, who had suddenly developed an entirely new character, would not listen to it. During his short sojourn in India, he had picked up a wonderful amount of useful Hindostani words, which he strung together recklessly, and by means of some of them, accompanied by frantic gesticulation, he informed all present that "*he* was not going to sleep under a cart, but was resolved to spend the night at Karwassa. He would walk there."

After a short, but stormy, altercation, my cousin carried his point, and set out, accompanied (with great reluctance) by Jones, Nuddoo the shikari, and myself. Algy took command of the party, and got over the ground at an astonishing pace. The yellow light faded and faded, and was succeeded by a grey deathly pallor that rapidly settled down upon the whole face of nature. We marched two and two, along the grass-grown, neglected roads, glancing askance at every bush, at every big tuft of elephant grass (at least, I speak for myself). At last, to my intense relief, the smoke and fires of a village came in view. It proved to be Karwassa—Karwassa strongly entrenched behind its mud walls and a bamboo palisade. After some parley we were admitted by the chowkidar (or watchman), and presently surrounded by the villagers, a poverty-stricken crew, with a depressed, hunted look.

"Once more a party of sahibs come to shoot the man-eaters," they exclaimed. "Ah, many sahibs had come and come and gone, and naught availed them against the Bagh. He was no Janwar—but an evil spirit."

"But two days ago," said the Malgoozar, or head-man—a high-caste Brahmin, with a high-bred face—"he had taken a boy from before his mother's eyes, as she tilled the patch of vegetables; the screams of the child—he had heard them himself. Ah, ye-yo!"

And he shook his enormous orange turban, and his handsome dignified head, in a truly melancholy fashion. "Moreover, the tiger had taken the woman's husband—there was not a house in the village that had not lost at least one inmate."

"Why did they not go away?" I asked.

"Yea—truly, others had abandoned their houses and lands, and fled—but to what avail? The thing was not a Janwar, but a devil."

A murmur of assent signified that the villagers had accepted their scourge, with the apathetic fatalism of their race. We were presently conducted to an empty hut, provided with broad string beds—and a light. Our Christmas dinner was simple; it consisted of chuppatties and well water, and our spirits were in keeping with our fare; the surrounding misery had infected us. We were even indebted for our present lodgings to the tiger—he had dined upon its former tenant about a month previously. By all accounts he was old, and lame of one hind leg, and had discovered that a human being is a far easier prey than nimble cattle, or fleeting deer. He had studied the habits of his victims, and would stalk the unwary, or the loiterer, like a great cat. Alas! many were the tragedies; with success he had grown bolder, and even broad noonday, and the interior of the village itself, now afforded no protection from his horrible incursions.

The next morning our carts arrived, and we unpacked (the salt, tea, and corkscrew had been forgotten). Afterwards we set out to explore, first the vegetable patches, then the meagre crops, and finally we were shown the dry river bed, the tiger's high-road to Karwassa. We tracked him easily in the soft, fine, white sand; there were his three huge paws, and a fainter impression of the fourth. Also, there were marks of something dragged, and several dark brown splashes; it was here that he had carried off the wife of one of our present guides, who had looked on,—being powerless to save her.

Needless to say, we were filled with a raging thirst for the blood of this beast—

Algy especially. He jawed, he bribed, he gesticulated, he held long conferences with the villagers, with Nuddoo the shikari—an active, leather-skinned man, with a cast in his left eye, who spoke English fluently, and wore a tiger charm. Algy accommodated himself to circumstances with astonishing facility. Most of the night we sat up in a machan, or platform in a tree, over a fat young buffalo, hoping to tempt the man-eater after dark. Subsequently Algy slept soundly on his native charpoy, breakfasted on milk and chuppatties, and sallied forth, gun on shoulder, to tramp miles over the surrounding country. He was indefatigable, and easily wore *me* out. As I frankly explained, I could not burn the candle at both ends, and sit curled up in a tree till two o'clock in the morning, and then walk down game that self-same afternoon. He never seemed to tire, and he left the champagne and whisky to us, and shot on milk or cold cocoa. His newly acquired Spartan taste declined our imported dainties (tinned and otherwise), and professed to prefer, in deference to our surroundings, a purely vegetable diet.

It was an odd fancy, which I made no effort to combat. Naturally there was more truffled turkey and *pâté de foie gras* and boar's head for *us*! Algy was a successful shot, and reaped the reward of his energy in respectable bags of black buck, hares, sand grouse, chickhira, bustard, peacock—no, though sorely tempted, he refrained from bagging the bird specially sacred to his hosts. Days and nights went by, and so far we were as unsuccessful as our forerunners. In spite of our fat and enticing young buffalo, whom we sometimes sat over from sunset until the pale wintry dawn glimmered along the horizon, we never caught one glimpse of the object of our expedition. Algy was restless, Nuddoo at his wits' end, whilst Jones had given up the quest as a bad job!

One evening we all gathered round the big fire in the village "chowk" (for the nights were chilly), having a "bukh" with the elders, and, being encompassed by a closely investing audience of the entire population—including, of course, infants in arms—our principal topic was the brute that had so successfully eluded us.

"He will never be caught save by one bait," remarked a venerable man, wagging his long white beard.

"And what is that, O my father?" I asked.

"A man or a woman," was the startling reply; "and those we cannot give."

"Yea, but we can!" cried a shrill voice. There was a sudden movement in the crowd, and a tall female figure broke out of the throng, and pushed her way into the open space and the full light of the fire. She wore the usual dark red petticoat, short-sleeved jacket, and blue cloth or veil over her head. This she suddenly tossed aside, and, as she stood revealed before us, her hair was dishevelled, her black eyes blazed with excitement; but she was magnificently handsome. No flat-faced Gond this, but a Marathi of six-and-twenty years of age—supremely beautiful.

"Protectors of the poor," she cried, flinging out her two modelled arms, jingling with copper bangles, "here am *I*. I am willing, and thou shalt give *me*. The shaitan has slain my man and my son. When the elephant is gone, why keep the goad? This devil of tigers has eaten more than one hundred of our people, and I gladly offer my life in exchange for his. Cattle! no"—with scorn. "He seeks not our flocks; he seeks *us*! Have we not learned that, above all, he prefers women folk and young? Therefore, behold I give myself"—looking round with a dramatic gesture of her hand—"to save all these."

"It is Sassi," muttered the Malgoozar, "the widow of Gitan. Since seven days her mind hath departed. She is mad."

"Nay, my father, but I am wise! Truly, it is the sahib's shikari who is foolish, and of but little wit. He knows not the ground. There is the stream close to the forest and the crops. The sahibs shall sit above in the old bher tree, with their guns. They shall tie me up below. Lo, I will sing, yea, loudly, and perchance the tiger will come. He is now seven days without food from our village. Surely he must be an-hungered. I will sing, and bring him to the great lords' feet—even to his death and mine. Then will my folk be avenged, and my name remembered—Sassi the Marathi, who gave her life for her people!"

She paused, and every eye was fixed upon her as she stood amidst a breathless silence, awaiting our answer, as immovable as a statue.

"Truly, what talk is so foolish as the talk of a woman?" began the Malgoozar, fretfully. "Small mouth, big speech——"

"Nay, my father," interrupted Nuddoo, eagerly, "but she speaks words of wisdom, and 'tis I that am the fool. The lord sahib returns in two days' time—and we have done naught."

As he spoke, his best eye was fixed on Sassi with an expression of ravenous greed not to be described. Apparently he saw the five hundred rupees now within a measurable distance!

"She can lure him, she shall stand on the stack of Bhoosa that pertains to Ruckoo, the chowkidar; she will sing—the nights are still. The Bagh will hear, he will come, and, ere he can approach, the sahibs will shoot him. After all"—with a contemptuous shrug—"it is but a mad woman and a widow."

"Nuddoo," shouted Algy, "if I ever hear you air those sentiments again, I'll shoot you. We don't want that sort of bait; and, if we did, I would sooner tie *you* up, than a woman and a widow."

Nuddoo's eager protestations, and Algy's expostulations, were loud and long, and during them a stern-faced old hag placed her hand on Sassi's shoulder, drew her out of the crowd, and the episode was closed.

Our expedition that night was, as usual, fruitless. We climbed into our tree platform, the now accustomed buffalo dozed in his place undisturbed. Evidently Algy's mind dwelt on the recent scene at the chowk, and he harangued me from time to time, in an excited whisper, on the subject of Sassi's heroism, her wonderful beauty, and Nuddoo's base suggestion. He was still whispering, when I fell asleep. And now it had come to our last day but one. Jones looked upon further effort as supreme folly. He wanted, for once, a night's unbroken rest, and at six o'clock we left him lying on his string bed, on the flat of his back, smoking cigarettes and reading a two-shilling novel—a novel dealing with smart folk in high life—a book that carried his thoughts far, far from a miserable mud village in the C.P. and its living scourge. How I envied Jones! I would thankfully have excused myself, but Algy was *my* cousin; he had taken command of the trip, and of me, ever since we had quitted the great trunk road—and I was entirely under his orders.

Nuddoo was not above accepting a hint; this time our machan was lashed into a big pepul tree on the border of the forest, and the edge of a stream that had its home in the hills. We were about two miles from Karwassa as the crow flies, and, as we were rather early, we had ample time to look about us; the scene was a typical landscape in the Central Provinces. To our left lay the hills, covered with dense woodlands, from whose gloomy depths emerged the now shallow river, which trickled gently past us over its bed of dark blue rock and gravel. Beyond the stream, and exactly facing us, lay a vast expanse of grain—*jawarri, gram,* and vetches—as far as the eye could reach, the monotonous stretch being broken, here and there, by a gigantic and solitary jungle tree. To the right, and on our side of the bank, was an exquisite sylvan glade, a suitable spot to which the forest fairies might issue invitations to the neighbouring elves to "come and dance in the moonbeams." Between the great trees, the waving crops, and the murmuring brook, I could almost have imagined myself in the midlands of England—save for certain tracks in the sand beneath our tree. Its enormous roots were twisted among rocks and boulders, and, where a spit of gravel ran out into the clear water, were many footprints, which showed where the bear, hyena, tiger, and jackal had come to slake their thirst. I noticed that Nuddoo seemed restless and strange, and that his explanations and answers were incoherent, not to say foolish.

"This looks a likely enough place," said Algy, with the confidence of a man who had been after tiger for years. "But, I say, Nuddoo, where's the chap with the buffalo—where is our tie-up?"

"Buffalo never started yet—plenty time—coming by-and-by, at moonrise," stammered Nuddoo; and, as I climbed into the machan, and he took his place next me, with our rifles, it struck me that Nuddoo was not sober. He smelt powerfully of raw whisky—our whisky—his lips were cracked and dry, and his hand shook visibly. What had he been doing?

"It will be an awful sell if there is no tie-up, and the tiger happens to go by," said Algy, irritably.

"The gara will be here without fail, your honour's worship. It will be all right, I swear it by the head of my son. Moreover, we will get the tiger—to-night he touches his last hour."

There was no question that Nuddoo, for the first time in my experience, was very drunk indeed. Presently the full moon rose up and illuminated the lonely landscape, the haunted jungle, the crops, the glade, and turned the forest stream to molten silver. It was nine o'clock, and, whilst Nuddoo slumbered, Algy and I held our breath, as we watched a noble sambur stag come and drink below us. He was succeeded by an old boar, next came a hyena; it was a popular resort; in short, every animal appeared but the one we wanted—and *he* was undoubtedly in the neighbourhood, for the deer seemed uneasy.

It was already after ten, and Algy was naturally impatient, and eagerly looking out for our devoted "gara." He and I were bending forward, listening anxiously; the forest behind us seemed full of stealthy noises, but we strained our ears in vain for the longed-for sound of buffalo hoofs advancing from the front. Nuddoo still slept soundly, and at last Algy, in great exasperation, leant over and shook him roughly.

"Ay," he muttered, in a sleepy grunt, "it is all right, sahib, the gara will come without fail."

Even whilst he spoke, we heard, not fifty yards away, the voice of a woman singing in the glade, and Nuddoo now started up erect, and began to tremble violently.

It was light as day, as we beheld Sassi advancing slowly in our direction, singing in a loud clear voice an invocation to Mahadeo the Destroyer!

When she had approached within earshot she halted, and, raising her statuesque face to her namesake the moon, chanted—

"O great lords in the pepul tree, whereto Nuddoo, the drunkard, hath led you,
Behold, according to my promise, lo! I have come.
I sing to my gods, and perchance I will bring the tiger to your honours' feet."

For the space of three heart-beats, we remained motionless—paralyzed with horror,—and then Nuddoo, who was gibbering with most mysterious terror, gave me a sudden and an involuntary push.

There, to the left, was *something* coming rapidly through the crops! The grain parted and waved wildly as it passed; in a moment a huge striped animal, the size of a calf, had crossed the river with a hurried limp.

"Kubberdar! Bagh! Bagh!" roared Algy to the woman. To me, "You've got him!"

Undoubtedly it was *my* shot, but I was excessively flurried—it was new to me to have a human life hanging on my trigger; as he sprang into the open glade I fired—and missed. I heard my cousin draw in his breath hard; I saw the woman turn and face us. The tiger's spring and Algy's shot seemed simultaneous; as the echo died away, there was not another sound—the great brute lay dead across the corpse of his victim. I was now shaking as much as Nuddoo; my bad aim had had a frightful result. Before I could scramble down, Algy, with inconceivable rashness, was already beside the bodies, where they lay in the middle of the glade—the monster stretched above his voluntary prey.

The news spread to the village in some miraculous manner. Had the birds of the air carried the great tidings? The entire community were instantly roused by the intelligence. Man, woman, yea, and child, came streaming forth, beating tom-toms and shouting themselves hoarse with joy. They collected about the tiger—who was evidently of far more account than the woman—they kicked him, cursed him, spat on him, and secretly stole his whiskers for a charm against the evil eye. They thrummed the tom-toms madly as they marched round and round Algy—the hero of the hour.

Nuddoo had now entirely forgotten his tremors, he was almost delirious with excitement; the five hundred rupees were his, he could live on them—and on his reputation as the slayer of the great Karwassa man-eater—for the remainder of his existence. He talked till he frothed at the corners of his mouth, he boasted here, he boasted there. He declared that "*he* had encouraged Sassi, and given her an appointment as the gara, or tie-up. Yea, she had spoken truly—there was no other means!"

Released from his honours and the transports of the tom-toms, these fatal words fell on Algy's ears, and he went straight for Nuddoo. What he said or did, I know not, but this I know, that from that moment I never saw Nuddoo again until weeks later, when he came to me by stealth in Kori, exceedingly humble and sober, and received, according to Algy's instructions, "five hundred rupees; but if he asks you for a chit," wrote Algy, "kick him out of the compound."

The tiger was big and heavy, he required twenty coolies to carry him back to Karwassa—for his last visit. Sassi was borne on the frame of our machan—ere she was placed there, an old hag covered the beautiful dead face with her veil, and slipped off her sole ornaments, the copper bangles, in a business-like fashion.

"Give me one of those," said Algy, who was standing by. "I will pay you well. Were you her mother?"

"Her grandmother," replied the crone. "She was mad. Lo, now she is gone, I shall surely starve!" and she began to whimper for the first time. Truly, she knew this sahib was both rich and open-handed.

Algy and I slept soundly for the remainder of that eventful night; but it is my opinion that the villagers never went to rest at all. The moment we set foot in the street the next morning, a vast crowd surged round my cousin; every one of them carried a string of flowers or—highest compliment—a gilded lime. Women brought their children, from the youngest upwards, and Algy was soon the centre of the village nursery. All these little people were solemnly requested "to look well upon that honoured lord, and to remember when they were old, and to tell it to their children, that their own eyes had rested on the great sahib who had killed the shaitan of Karwassa."

Algy was loaded with honours and flowers; I must confess that he bore them modestly, and he, on his side, paid high tribute to Sassi the Marathi. He commanded that she should have a splendid funeral. The most costly pyre that was ever seen in those parts was erected, the memory of the oldest inhabitant was vainly racked to recall anything approaching its magnificence. The village resources, and the resources of three other hamlets, were strained to the utmost tension to provide sandal-wood, oil, jewels, and dress. If Algy's London "pals" could hear of him spending fifty pounds on the burning of a native woman, how they would laugh and chaff him! I hinted as much, and got a distinctly nasty reply. He was quite right; roughing it *had* a bad effect upon his temper. At sundown the whole population assembled by the river bank to witness the obsequies of Sassi the widow of Gitan; they marvelled much (and so did I) to behold my cousin standing by, bare-headed, during the entire ceremony.

We set out on our return journey that same evening—travelling by moonlight had no dangers now! Algy distributed immense largesse among his friends, viz. the entire community (he also paid all our expenses like a prince). He and the inhabitants of Karwassa parted with many good wishes and mutual reluctance; indeed, a body of them formed a running accompaniment to us for nearly a dozen miles. Our spoil, the tiger's skin, was a poor specimen. The stripes had a dull, faded appearance; but it measured, without stretching, a good honest ten feet from nose to tip of tail. Once we were out of the jungle, and back in the land of bungalows, daily posts, and baker's bread, Algy relapsed from a keen and intrepid sportsman into an indolent, drawling dandy. The day after our return to Kori, he took leave of me in these remarkable words—

"Well, good-bye, Perky. You are not a bad sort, though you are not much of a chap to shoot or rough it. However, I have to thank you for taking me off the beaten track, and showing me something which I shall never forget,—and that was entirely out of the common."

"The Missus."

A Dog Tragedy.

When the Royal British Skirmishers were quartered in Bombay, their second in command was Major Bowen, a spare, grizzled, self-contained little soldier, who lived alone in one of those thatched bungalows that resemble so many monstrous mushrooms, bordering the racecourse. "The Major," as he was called *par excellence,* was best described by negatives. He was not married. He was not a ladies' man. Nor was he a sportsman; nor handsome, young, rich, nor even clever—in short, he was not remarkable for anything except, perhaps, his dog. No one could dispute the fact that Major Bowen was the owner of an uncommon animal. He and this dog had exchanged into "the Skirmishers" from another regiment six years previously, and though the pair were at first but coldly received, they adapted themselves so admirably to their new surroundings that ere long they had gained the esteem and goodwill of both rank and file; and, as time wore on, there actually arose an ill-concealed jealousy of their old corps, and a disposition to ignore the fact that they had not always been part and parcel of the gallant Skirmishers. Although poor, and having but little besides his pay, the Major was liberal—both just and generous; and if he was mean or close-fisted with any one, that person's name was Reginald Bowen. He had an extremely lofty standard of honour and of the value of his lightest word. He gave a good tone to the mess, and though he was strict with the youngsters, they all liked him. Inflexible as he could look on parade or in the orderly-room, elsewhere he received half the confidences of the regiment; and many a subaltern had been extricated from a scrape, thanks to the little Major's assistance—monetary and otherwise. He was a smart officer and a capital horseman, and here was another source of his popularity. He lent his horses and ponies, with ungrudging good faith, to those impecunious youths who boasted but the one hard-worked barrack "tat;" and many a happy hour with hounds, or on the polo-ground, was spent on the back of the Major's cattle. Major Bowen did not race or hunt, and rarely played polo; in fact, he was not much interested in anything—although upwards of forty, he was supremely indifferent to his dinner!—the one thing he really cared about was his *dog*: a sharp, well-bred fox-terrier, with bright eyes and lemon-coloured ears,—who, in spite of the fact that her original name was "Minnie," had been known as "the Missus" for the last five years. This name was given to her in joke, and in acknowledgment of her accomplishments; the agreeable manner in which she did the honours of her master's bungalow, and the extraordinary care she took of him, and all his property. It was truly absurd to see this little creature—of at most sixteen pounds' weight—gravely lying, with crossed paws, in front of the Major's sixteen hands "waler," whilst he was going round barracks, or occupied in the orderly-room. Her pose of self-importance distinctly said, "The horse and syce are in *my* charge!"

She went about the compound early every morning, and rigorously turned out vagrants, suspicious-looking visitors to the servants' quarters, and all dogs and goats! She accompanied her master to mess, and fetched him home, no matter how late the hour—and through the rains (and they are no joke in Bombay) it was just the same; there was the chokedar, with his mackintosh and lantern; and there was also, invariably, the shivering, sleepy little Missus. It was of no avail to tie her up at home; not only were her heartrending howls audible for a quarter of a mile, but on one occasion she actually arrived under the dinner-table, chain and all, to the discomfort of the Colonel's legs, the great scandal of the mess-sergeant, and her own everlasting disgrace! So she was eventually suffered—like wilful woman—to have her way. Her master's friends were her friends, and took the Missus quite seriously—but she drew the line at dogs. It must be admitted that her manners to her own species were—not nice. She had an unladylike habit of suddenly sitting down when she descried one afar off, and sniffing the, so to speak, tainted air, that was nothing more nor less than a deliberate insult to any animal with the commonest self-respect; many a battle was fought, many a bite was given and received. The Missus was undeniably accomplished; she fetched papers and slippers, gave the paw, and in the new style—on a level with her head, walked briskly on her hind legs, could strum on the piano, and sing, accompanying herself to a clear, somewhat shrill, soprano. There was a little old pianette in the Major's sitting-room, on which she performed amid great applause. It was *not* true that the instrument had been purchased solely for her use, or that she practised industriously for two hours a day. No—the pianette had been handed over to her master by a young man (who had subsequently gone to the dogs) as the only available payment of a sum the Major had advanced for him. Battered old tin kettle as it was, that despised piano had cost one hundred pounds! But no one dreamt of *this* when they laughed at its shortcomings. The Missus was passionately fond of music, and escorted her owner to the band; but she escorted him almost everywhere—to the club, round the barracks, the racecourse, to church—here she was ignominiously secured in the syce's "cupra," as she had a way of stealthily peeping in at the various open doors, and endeavouring to focus her idol, which manœuvre—joined with her occasional assistance in the chanting—proved a little trying to the gravity of the congregation. Of course she went to the hills—where she had an immense acquaintance; she had also been on active service on the Black Mountain, and when one night a prowling Afridi crept on his hands and knees into the Major's tent, he found himself unexpectedly pinned by a set of sharp teeth,—he carried the mark of that bite to his grave.

Major Bowen was not the least ashamed of his affection for his dog. She was his weak point—even the very Company's dhobies approached him through her favour. He was president of the mess, and in an excellent manner had officiated for years in that difficult and thankless office; a good man of business—prompt, clear-headed, methodical, and conscientious. No scamping of accounts, no peculations overlooked, a martinet to the servants, and possibly less loved than feared. But this is a digression from the Missus. Her master was foolishly proud of her good looks—very sensitive respecting her little foibles (which he clumsily endeavoured to conceal), and actually touchy about her age!

When the Missus had her first, and only, family, it was quite a great local event. The Major's establishment was turned completely upside down; there was racing and chasing to procure two milch goats for the use of the infants and their mother, and a most elegant wadded basket was provided as a cradle. But, alas! the Missus proved a most indifferent parent. She deserted her little encumbrances at the end of one day, and followed her master to the Gymkana ground. He was heartily ashamed of her, and positively used to remain indoors for the sake of keeping up appearances. He could not go to the club, and have the Missus waiting conspicuously outside with the pony, when all the world knew that she had no business to be there, but had four young and helpless belongings squealing for her at home! She accorded them but little of her company, and appeared to think that her nursery cares were entirely the affair of the two milch goats! One of her neglected children pined, and dwindled, and eventually died, was placed in a cigar-box, and buried in a neat little grave under a rose-bush in the compound, whilst its unnatural mamma looked on from afar off, a totally uninterested spectator! The three survivors were handsome puppies, and the Major exhibited them with pride to numerous callers, and finally bestowed them among his friends (entirely to please their mother, whom they bored to death). They were gratefully accepted, not merely on their own merits, but also as being a public testimonial of their donor's high opinion and esteem.

* * * * *

It was towards the end of the monsoon, when the compound was almost afloat, and querulous frogs croaked in every corner of the verandahs, that Major Bowen became seriously ill with low malarious fever. He had been out ten years—"five years too long," the doctor declared; "he must go home at once, and never return to India." This was bad news for the regiment, and still worse for the invalid, who helped a widowed sister with all he could spare from his colonial allowances. There would not be much margin on English pay!

He was dangerously ill in that lofty, bare, whitewashed bedroom in Infantry Lines. He would not be the first to die there. No,—not by many. His friends were devoted and anxious. The Missus was devoted and distracted. She lay all day long at the foot of his cot, watching and listening, and following his slightest movement with a pair of agonized eyes.

At length there was a change—and for the better. The patient was promoted into a cane lounge in the sitting-room, to solids, and to society—as represented by half the regiment. He looked round his meagrely furnished little room with interested eyes. There was not a speck of dust to be seen, everything was in its place, to the letter-weight on the writing-table, and the old faded photos in their shabby leather frames. Missus's basket was pushed into a far corner. She had not used it for weeks. He and Missus were going home, and would soon say good-bye for ever to the steep-roofed thatched bungalow, the creaking cane chairs, the red saloo purdahs, to the verandahs, embowered in pale lilac "railway" creeper, to the neat little garden—to the regiment—to Bombay. Their passages were taken. They were off in the *Arcadia* in three days.

* * * * *

That afternoon, the Major had all his kit and personal property paraded in his sitting-room, in order that the packing of his belongings (he was a very tidy man) should take place under his own eyes. The bearer was in attendance, and with him his slave and scapegoat—the chokra.

The bearer was a stolid, impassive-looking Mahomedan, with a square black beard, and a somewhat sullen eye.

"Abdul," said his master, as his gaze travelled languidly from one neatly folded pile of clothes to another—from guns in cases to guns not in cases, to clocks, revolvers, watches, candlesticks—the collection of ten years, parting gifts, bargains, and legacies—"you have been my servant for six years, and have served me well. I have twice raised your wages, and you have made a very good thing out of me, I believe, and can, no doubt, retire and set up a ticca gharry, or a shop. I am going away, and never coming back, and I want to give you something of mine as a remembrance—something to remember me by, you understand?"

The bearer deliberately unfolded his arms, and salaamed in silence.

"You may choose anything you like out of this room," continued the Major, with unexampled recklessness.

Abdul's eyes glittered curiously—it was as if a torch had suddenly illumined two inky-black pools.

"Sahib never making joke—sahib making really earnest?"—casting on him a glance of almost desperate eagerness. The glance was lost on his master, whose attention was fixed on a discarded gold-laced tunic and mess-jacket.

"Of course," he said to himself, "Abdul will choose them," for gold lace is ever dear to a native heart, it sells so well in the bazaar, and melts down to such advantage.

"Making earnest!" repeated the invalid, irritably. "Do I ever do otherwise? Look sharp, and take your choice."

"Salaam, sahib," he answered, and turned quickly to where the Missus was coiled up in a chair. "I take my choice of anything in this room. Then I take—the—dog."

"The—*dog*!" repeated her owner, with a half-stupefied air.

"Verily, I am fond of Missy. Missy fond of master. The dog and I will remember the sahib together, when he is far away."

The sahib felt as if some one had suddenly plunged a knife in his heart. In Abdul's bold gaze, in Abdul's petition, he, too late, recalled the solemn (but despised) warning of a brother-officer:

"That bearer of yours is a vindictive brute; you got his son turned out of the mess, and serve him right, for a drunken, thieving hound! But sleek as he looks, Abdul will have it in for you yet;" and this was accomplished, when he said, "The dog and I, sahib, will remember you together."

Major Bowen was still desperately weak, and he had just been dealt a crushing blow; but the spirit that holds India was present in that puny, wasted frame, and, with a superhuman effort, he boldly confronted the two natives—the open-mouthed, gaping chokra, the respectfully exultant bearer—and said, "Atcha" (that is to say, "good"), "it is well;" and then he feebly waved to the pair to depart from him, for he was tired.

Truly it was anything but "good." It seemed the worst calamity that could have befallen him. He was alone, and face to face with a terrible situation. He must either forfeit his word, or his dog,—which was it to be?

In all his life, to the best of his knowledge, he had never broken his faith, and now to do it to a native!—that was absolutely out of the question. But his dog—his friend—his companion—with whom he never meant to part, as long as she lived (for *she* had given her to him). He sat erect, and looked over at the Missus, where she lay curled up; her expressive eyes met his eagerly.

Little, O Missus, do you guess the fatal promise that has just been made, nor how largely it concerns *you*. Her master lay back with a groan, and turned his face away from the light, a truly miserable man! His faithful Missus!—to have to part with her to one of the regiment would have been grief enough; but to a Mahomedan, with their unconcealed scorn of dogs! He must have been mad when he made that rash offer; but then, in justification, his common sense urged, "How was he to suppose that Abdul would choose anything but a silver watch, a gun, or the worth of fifty rupees?" Major Bowen was far from being an imaginative man, but as he lay awake all night long, and listened to the wild roof-cats stealing down the thatch, and heard them pattering back at dawn, one mental picture stood out as distinctly as if he was looking at it with his bodily sight, and it was actually before him.

A low, squalid mud hut in a bazaar; a native string bed, and tied to it by a cord—*the Missus*. "The Missus," with thin ribs, a staring coat, and misery depicted on her little face, the sport of the children and the flies—starved, forlorn, heartbroken—dumbly wondering what had happened to her master, and why he had so cruelly deserted her! Oh, when was he coming to fetch her? Not knowing, she was at least spared *this*—that he would never come.

What an insane promise! As he recalled it, he clenched his hands in intolerable agony. Why did he not *offer* his watch—his rifle? he would give Abdul a thousand rupees, gladly, to redeem the dog, but his inner consciousness assured him that Abdul, thanks to him, was already well-to-do, and that his revenge was worth more to him than money. This would not be the case with most natives, but he knew, to his cost, that Abdul's was a stern, tenacious, relentless nature. At one moment, he had decided to poison the Missus with his own hands—prussic acid was speedy; at another, he had resolved to remain in India, doctors or no doctors.

"And sacrifice your life?" again breathed common sense. "Die for a dog!" True, but the dog was not a dog to him. She was his comrade, his sympathizer, his friend. Meanwhile, the object of all these mental wrestlings and agonies slept the sleep of the just, innocent, and ignorant; but in any case, it is a question if a dog's anxieties ever keep it awake. Her master never closed his eyes; he saw the dawn glimmer through the bamboo chicks; he saw Abdul, the avenger, appear with his early tea, and Abdul found him in high fever; perhaps Abdul was not greatly surprised!

Friends and brother-officers flocked in that day, and sat with the Major, and they noted with concern that he looked worse than he had done at any period of his illness. His naturally pinched face was worn and haggard to a startling degree. Moreover, in spite of the news of the high prices his horses had fetched, he was terribly "down," and why? A man going home, after ten years of India, is generally intolerably cheerful. They did their best to enliven him, these good-hearted comrades, and—unfailing topic of interest—they discoursed volubly and incessantly of the Missus.

"She is looking uncommonly fit," said young Stradbrooke, the owner of one of her neglected children. "She knows she is going to England. She was quite grand with me just now! She hates boating like the devil! I wonder how she will stand fourteen days at sea?"

There was a perceptible silence after this question, and then the Major said in a queer voice—

"She is—not—going."

"Not going?" An incredulous pause, and then some one exclaimed: "Come, Major, you know you would just as soon leave your head behind."

"All the same—I am leaving her——"

"And which of us is to have her?" cried the Adjutant. "Take notice, all, that I speak first. You won't pass over me, sir. Missus and I were always very chummy, and I want her to look after my chargers and servants, fetch my slippers, bring me home from mess—and to take care of me and keep me straight."

"I have already given her away to— —" the rest of the sentence seemed to stick in the Major's throat, and his face worked painfully.

"Away to whom?" repeated young Stradbrooke. "Say it's to *me*, sir. I've one of the family already—and Missus likes me. I know her pet biscuits, and there are heaps of rats in my stables—such whoppers!"

"Given her—to the bearer—Abdul," he answered, stoutly enough, though there was still a little nervous quivering of the lower lip.

If the ceiling had parted asunder and straightway tumbled down on their heads, the Major's audience would not have been half so much dumfoundered. For a whole minute they sat agape, and then one burst out—

"I say, Major, it's a joke—you would not give her out of the regiment; she is on the *strength*."

"She is promised," replied the Major, in a sort of husky whisper.

Every one knew that the Major's promises were a serious matter, and after this answer there ensued a long dismayed silence. The visitors eventually turned the topic, and tried to talk of other matters—the last gazette, the new regimental ribbon, of anything but of what every mind was full, to wit, "the Missus."

The news respecting her bestowal created quite a sensation that evening at the mess—far more than that occasioned by a newly announced engagement, for there was an element of mystery about *this* topic. Why had the Missus been given away?

"Bowen must be off his chump," was the general verdict, "poor old chap, to give the dog to that rascal Abdul, of all people!" (One curious feature in Anglo-Indian life, is the low opinion people generally entertain of their friends' servants.) "The proper thing was, of course, to buy the dog, and keep her in the regiment; and when the Major came to his right senses, how glad he would be, dear old man!"

The Adjutant waylaid Abdul in the road, and said, curtly—

"Is this true, about the dog?—that your sahib has given her to you?"

Abdul salaamed. How convenient and non-committal is that gesture!

"What will you take for her?"

"I never selling master's present," rejoined the bearer, with superb dignity.

"What does a nigger want with a dog?" demanded the officer, scornfully.

"Well, then, swop her—*that* won't hurt your delicate sense of honour. I'll get you an old pariah out of the bazaar, and give you fifty rupees to buy him a collar!"

"I have refused to-day one thousand rupees for the Missy," said Abdul, with increased hauteur.

"You lie, Abdul," said the officer, sternly; "or else you have been dealing with a stark, staring madman."

"I telling true, Captain Sahib. I swear by the beard of the Prophet."

"Who made the offer?"

"Major Bone"—the natives always called him "Major Bone."

"Great Scott! Poor dear old chap" (to himself): "I had no idea he was so badly touched. It is well he is going home, or it would be a case of four orderlies and a padded room. So much for this beastly country!" Then to Abdul, "Look here; don't say a word about that offer, and come over to my quarters, and I'll give you some dibs—the sun has been too much for your sahib—and mind you be kind to the Missus; if not, I'll come and shoot her, and thrash you within an inch of your life."

"Gentlemen Sahib never beating servants. Sahib touch me, I summon in police-court, and I bring report to regimental commanding officer. Also, I going my own country, Bareilly, and I never, never selling kind master's present."

"I know lots of Sahibs in a pultoon (*i.e.* regiment) at Bareilly, and I shall get them to look out for you and the dog, Mr. Abdul. You treat 'kind master's present' well, and it will be well with you,—if not, by Jove, you will find that I have got a long arm. I am a man of my word, so keep your mouth shut about the Major. To-night my bearer will give you ten rupees." And he walked on.

"Bowen must be in a real bad way, when he gives his beloved dog to a native, and next day wants to buy it back for a thousand rupees," said Captain Young to himself. "I thought he looked queer yesterday, but I never guessed that he was as mad as twenty hatters."

* * * * *

The hour of the Major's departure arrived; he had entreated, as a special favour, that no one would come to see him off. This request was looked upon as more of his eccentricity, and not worthy of serious consideration; he would get all right as soon as he was at sea, and the officers who were not on duty hurried down to see the last of their popular comrade. He drove up late, looking like death, his face so withered, drawn, and grey, and got out of a gharry, promptly followed by Abdul, carrying the Missus. The steam-launch lay puffing and snorting at the steps—the other passengers were aboard—there was not a moment to lose. The Major bade each and all a hurried farewell; he took leave of the Missus last. She was still in Abdul's arms, and believed in her simple dog mind that her master was merely bound for one of those detestable sails up the harbour. As she offered him an eager paw, little did she guess that it was good-bye for ever, or that she was gazing after him for the last time, as he feebly descended the steps and took his place in the tender that was to convey him to the P. and O. steamer.

He watched the crowd of friends wildly waving handkerchiefs; but he watched, above all, with a long, long gaze of inarticulate grief, a dark turbaned figure, that stood conspicuously apart, with a small white object in his arms: watched almost breathlessly, till it faded away into one general blur. The Bengal civilian who sat next to Major Bowen in the tender, stared at him in contemptuous astonishment. He had been twenty-five years in the country (mitigating his exile with as much furlough—sick, privilege, and otherwise—as he could possibly obtain), and this was the first time he had seen a man quit the shores of India—with *tears in his eyes*!

The Betrayal of Shere Bahadur.

I am merely the wife of a British subaltern, whereas my aunt Jane is the consort of a commissioner. One must go to India, to realize the enormous and unfathomable gulf which yawns between these two positions.

Take, for instance, that important difference—the difference in pay. On the first of each month, Aunt Jane's lord and master receives several thousand and odd rupees—a heavy load for two staggering peons to carry from the treasury—whereas my husband's poor little pittance, of two hundred and fifty-six rupees and odd annas, our bearer swings in a lean canvas bag, and in one hand, with an air of jaunty contempt!

At dinner-parties and other grand functions, I see my aunt's round-shouldered back, and well-known yellow satin, leading the van, with her hand on the host's arm, whilst I humbly bring up the rear—one of the last joints in the tail of precedence.

Afterwards—after coffee, conversation, and music—not a woman in the room may venture to stir, until my little fat relative has "made the move" and waddled off to her carriage. Mr. Radcliffe, my uncle by marriage, rules over a large district; he is a stout, puffy, imposing-looking man, attended by much pomp and circumstance, and many scarlet-clad chuprassis. His wife rules him—as well as the station; manages every one's affairs, acts as the censor of public morals, and may be implicitly relied upon to utter the disagreeable things that *ought* to be said, but that no one but herself is willing to say. The Radcliffes have no family, and therefore she has ample time to indulge her fine powers of observation, organization, and conversation. When I married, and was about to come to India, a year ago, my people remarked on an average once a week—

"If you are going to Luckmee, you will be quite close to your aunt Jane at Rajapore, and only think how delightful that will be for you!" but I was by no means so confident of this supreme future joy. Rajapore is a large mixed military and civil station; Luckmee is on the same line of rail, a run of a couple of hours; a small and insignificant cantonment, which looks up to Rajapore as its metropolis, and does all its shopping there. No, I did not find it at all delightful, being within such easy hail of Aunt Jane. She made unexpected descents—as a rule, early in the morning—driving up from the station in a rickety "ticca gharry," to spend what she called "a good long day." First of all, she went over the bungalow precisely as if it was to let furnished, and she was the incoming tenant; then she cross-examined me closely, read my home letters, looked at my bazaar account, sniffed at my new frocks, snubbed my friends, and departed by the last train in the highest spirits, leaving me struggling with the idea that I was *still* a rather troublesome schoolgirl in short frocks and a pig-tail. Now and then I returned the visit—by command—drove with Aunt Jane in her state barouche, in which she sat supported by a pair of rather faded Berlin wool cushions, great eyesores to my critical English taste, which largely discounted the fine carriage, big bay walers, fat coachman (an Indian Jehu of any pretension must be corpulent), the running syces, and splendid silver-mounted chowries or yâk tails.

I also was present at various heavy tiffins and dinners, in the capacity of deputy assistant hostess and niece. I had come in now, to wait upon Aunt Jane and "take leave," as she was just off to England, and had imperatively summoned me to report myself ere she started. I found the great square white bungalow externally gay with *Bignonia vinusta,* internally in the utmost confusion. The hall was littered with straw and bits of newspapers, the drawing-room was full of packing-cases, half the contents of the cellar were paraded on the floor, and dozens of tins of "Europe" stores were also on review, all being for sale. Aunt Jane was seated at a writing-table, revising lists with a rapid pen.

"You discover me," she exclaimed, offering a plump cheek, "sitting like Marius among the ruins of Carthage."

I was dumb. I had no idea until now that Marius was a stout little elderly woman, wearing a shapeless grey wide-awake and blue spectacles.

"I feel almost fit for the poggle khana (mad-house)," she continued. "Just look here! Here is my list of furniture, come back from making the round of the station, and all that has been taken is a watering-pot, six finger-glasses, and a pie-dish!" (The truth was that people were tired of my aunt's lists.) "And here are dozens of servants clamouring for chits—and a man waiting to buy the cows. I wish to goodness some one would buy your uncle's shikar camel,"—reading aloud from list,—"'young, strong, easy trot and walk, with saddle, Rs. 200.' Your uncle is going to chum with Mr. Jones. He does not intend shooting this season—even *he* finds it an expensive pursuit," this in a significant parenthesis. "I've not put away the ornaments, nor sold off my stores, nor packed one of my own things."

I muttered some sympathetic remark, but I knew that Aunt Jane enjoyed these "earthquakings" immensely. She was constantly uprooting her establishment, and taking what she called "a run home."

"And you go on Monday?" I inquired.

"Yes, child; though I don't believe I shall ever be ready. Your mother, of course, will want to know how you are? I must candidly tell her that you are looking dreadfully pasty. Ah! I see you have got a parcel."

"Only a very little one," I pleaded apologetically.

"Well, well, I suppose I must *try* and take it; and now what are your plans?"

"Tom has got two months' leave, and Charlie is coming up from Madras; we are going away on a trip into the real jungle."

"For what?" she asked tartly.

"Well, to see something different from the routine of cantonment life, something different from the band-stand and D.W.P. pattern church—to see *real* India."

"What folly! Real India, indeed!" she snorted; "as if you would *ever* see it! It makes me wild to hear of people talking, and worse still, writing about India, as if one person could grasp even a small corner of it. Here am I, twenty-five years in the country, speaking the language fluently, and what do I know?" she paused dramatically. "The bazaar prices, the names of the local trees and flowers, the rents of the principal houses up at Simla." (I have reason to believe that my aunt did herself gross injustice; she knew the private affairs of half the civilians in the provinces, and was on intimate terms with their "family skeletons.") "As to the character of the people! I cannot even fathom my own ayah, and she is with me eleven years."

"I believe some people know a great deal about India," I ventured to protest.

"Stuff!" she interrupted. "One person may know a little of one part of the continent, but there are twenty Indias!—all different, with different climates, customs, and people. What resemblance is there between a Moplah on the west coast and a Leucha from Darjeeling, a little stunted Andamanese and a Sikh; a Gond from the C.P. and a Pathan from the frontier; a Bengali Baboo and a bold Rohilla?" (Aunt Jane was now mounted on her hobby, and I had nothing to do but to look and listen.) "Every one thinks his own little corner is India. You, as an officer's wife—the wife of a subaltern in a marching regiment"—(she always insisted on the prefix "marching")—"have better chances than a civilian, for they live in one groove; you are shot about from Colombo to Peshawar. However, much good it will do you, for you are naturally dull, and have no talent for observation."

"No, not like *you*, Aunt Jane," I ventured with mild sarcasm: was she not going home?

"And where are you bound for?" she pursued.

"About a hundred miles out, due north."

"That is the Merween district, I know it well. We were in that division years ago. Had you consulted *me*, before making your plans, your uncle might have arranged about elephants for you. It's too late now," with a somewhat triumphant air.

"But we don't want elephants," I protested; "we have our ponies."

"Id— —" correcting herself, "simpleton! I meant for shooting from. The district is full of long grass. Tom will get no deer, nor indeed any game on foot. You may have the shikar camel, if you like, for his keep, and the Oontwallah's pay—no?" as I shook my head emphatically. "Well, I can give you one tip: take plenty of tinned stores; the villages are scattered, and Brahmin. You won't get an egg, much less a fowl—at most a little ghee and flour; but I strongly advise you to take your own poultry, and a couple of milch goats, also *plenty* of quinine and cholera mixture; parts of the country are very marshy and unhealthy. I suppose you have tents? *We* cannot lend you any."

"Yes, we have three, thank you."

"And so your brother Charles is going with you! Tell him that *I* think he had much better have stayed quietly with his regiment, and worked for the higher standard—a boy only out two years. Of course *you* are paying his expenses?"

I nodded. Tom was moderately well off; though we were not rich, we were not exactly poor, and I always had a firm conviction that Aunt Jane would have liked me *much* better if I had been a pauper! As it was, she considered me dangerously independent.

"Of course you think you know your own business best!" removing her spectacles as she spoke, "but mark my words, you will find this trip a great deal more costly than you imagine. With us civilians it is different, a sort of royal progress; but with you—well, well," shaking her head, "you must buy your own experience!"

A week later we had set forth, Tom, Charlie, and myself. We took Aunt Jane's advice (it was all she had given us), and despatched our tents and carts twenty-four hours' ahead, so as to give them a good start. We cantered out after them, a fifteen-mile ride, the following day. It was my first experience of camp life, and perfectly delightful; the tent under the trees felt so cool and fresh, in comparison with a sun-baked bungalow. Our servants, who appeared quite at home, had built a mud fireplace, and were cooking the dinner; the milch goats were browsing, and the poultry picking about in the adaptable manner of an Indian bazaar fowl. Our next halt was to be twenty miles farther on, at an engineer's bungalow, which was splendidly situated between a forest swarming with game and a river teeming with fish. Here we intended to remain for some time; we should be in the territory of the Rajah of Betwa, and were bearers of a letter asking for his assistance, in the way of procuring provisions in the villages. At midday we halted for several hours in a mango tope, the home of thousands of monkeys, and went forward again about four o'clock. Our road was bordered at either side by a golden sea of gently waving crops, for we were in the heart of a great wheat country. Presently we passed through the town of Betwa, which chiefly consisted of a long dirty bazaar, an ancient fort, and a high mud wall, enclosing the palace of the rajah. About a mile beyond the outskirts, we beheld a cloud of yellow dust rapidly approaching.

"I'll bet ten to one it's the rajah," said Tom, as he abruptly pulled up his pony.

I felt intensely excited. I had never seen a real live rajah in my life; and I held myself in readiness for any amount of pomp and splendour, from milk-white arabs with gold trappings, to a glass coach. But what was this that I beheld, as we drew respectfully to one side? I could scarcely believe my own eyes, as there thundered by a most dilapidated waggonette, drawn by one huge bony horse and a pony, truly sorry steeds; the harness was tied up with rope, and even rags! Seated in front was a spare dark man, with a disagreeable expression, dressed in a stuff coat, the colour of Reckitt's blue, and a gold skull-cap. He salaamed to us in a condescending manner, and was presumably the rajah. A fat pock-marked driver held the reins; in the body of the waggonette were six men (the suite), and their united weight gave the vehicle a dangerous tilt backwards. The equipage was accompanied by four ragamuffins, with long spears, riding miserable old screws with bell-rope bridles. They kept up a steady tittuping canter, raising a cloud of suffocating dust, in which they presently vanished.

"I can't believe that *that* is a rajah, much less *our* rajah," I remarked to my companions.

"I can," said Tom, emphatically. "He looks what he is—an unmitigated scoundrel, and a miser. Did you notice how close his eyes were together? He is a rich man, too; is lord of the soil as far as your eyes can see. His grandfather owned a great deal more before the Mutiny, but it was shorn from him, and he was thankful to be left with an acre—or his life."

"Why?" asked Charlie and I in a breath.

"He came out of that bad business very badly. When the inhabitants of Luckmee were surprised, they sent their women and children to him for protection, he being, as they supposed, their very good friend; but he simply bundled them all out, and they were every one massacred. The rajah then believed that the mutineers would carry everything before them, but after the fall of Delhi he changed his tune, and sent on a charger the head of the chief leader in these parts—his own nephew, as it happened, but this is a detail—in order to make his peace. Of course, he saved his skin, but he had a bad record, and his grandson is a chip of the old block."

"Who told you all this?" I inquired.

"The collector. He says this man grinds down the ryots shamelessly, and does many a queer thing that ought to land him in a court of law. Here is the forest, and here, thank goodness, is *the* bungalow at last."

Our halting-place proved to be a thatched stone cottage, containing three rooms, and bath-rooms; there was a deep verandah all round, excellent servants' quarters and stables—in short, it was the beau idéal of a jungle residence. One verandah looked towards the forest, with its cool, dark recesses, the other commanded the river, and beyond it, faintly on the sky line, glimmered the snows.

The bungalow was surrounded by about twenty acres of park-like pasture, through which ran a public road leading to a fine bridge. We took in these details as we lounged about in the moonlight after dinner, and unanimously agreed that our present quarters were quite perfect in every respect.

The next day we fished—a nice, lazy, unexciting occupation. I sauntered home early in the afternoon—not being a particularly enthusiastic angler—and disposed myself in a comfortable deep straw chair in the verandah, in order to enjoy a novel and what I considered a well-earned cup of tea. As I reclined at my ease, devouring fiction and cake, sandwich fashion, my attention was arrested by a sound of loud crashing and smashing of branches in the usually death-like stillness of the forest. I sat erect, gazing intently at the violent storm among the leaves, expecting to see emerge a deer, a pig, or, at the very worst, a peacock! But after staring steadily for some time, I found that I was looking at the back of a remarkably tall elephant.

The ayah, who was also watching, pointed and called out, "Hathi, mem sahib, burra hathi," as if I did not know an elephant when I saw one!

Presently I descended the steps, strolled across the green, and pushed aside the bushes. There I beheld a lean native, all ribs and turban, busily engaged in baking his chupatties over a fire of sticks—a little wizened man, with a sharp cruel face, and close behind him stood a huge gaunt elephant, or rather the framework of one, for the animal was shockingly thin. Its poor backbone was as sharp as a razor; its skin hung in great wrinkles; its eye—an elephant's eye is small and ugly—this beast's eye gave expression to its whole body, and had a woful look of inarticulate misery, of almost desperate, human appeal.

The mahout stood up and salaamed, and forthwith he and I began to converse—that is to say, we made frantic endeavours to understand one another—the ayah, whose curiosity had dragged her forth, now and then throwing in a missing word.

"By my favour, it was the rajah's state elephant; he had also three others; he sent them into the forest to feed and to rest, when he did not require them. This, Shere Bahadur (brave lion), was the great processional elephant, and had a superb cloth-of-gold canopy that covered him from head to tail."

("Poor brute!" I said to myself, "otherwise he would be a terribly distressing spectacle.")

"Why is he so thin?" I demanded anxiously.

"Because he is old," was the ready answer, "more than one hundred years. He had been, so folk said, a war-elephant taken in battle. He was worth thousands and thousands of rupees once. He knew no fear, and no fatigue. Moreover, he was a great shikar elephant—many tigers had he faced"—and here the mahout proudly showed me the traces of some ancient scars—"even now the Sahib Log borrowed him as an honour."

"And what had he to eat?" I inquired.

"More than he could swallow—twelve large chupatties twice a day—this size"—holding his skinny arms wide apart—"also ghoor, and sugar-cane, and spice."

I looked about. I saw no sign of anything but a few branches of neem tree, and the preparations for the mahout's own meagre meal.

"Hazoor, he has had his khana—he has dined like a prince," reiterated the mahout. "Kuda ka Kussum," that is to say, "so help me God."

Nevertheless I remained incredulous. I went over to the bungalow and brought out a loaf, to the extreme consternation of our khansamah—we being forty miles from the nearest bazaar bakery—this I broke in two pieces, and presented it to Shere Bahadur, who seized it ravenously. Of course it was a mere crumb, and the wrinkled eager trunk was piteously held out for more; but more I dared not give, for I was in these days entirely under the yoke of my domestics! I related my little adventure during dinner—small episodes become great ones in the jungle, where we had no news, no dâk. Afterwards we took our usual stroll in the moonlight, and Charlie and I went to visit my new acquaintance. He was alone. The mahout was away, probably smoking at a panchayet in the nearest village. In a short time we were joined by Tom, who, as he came up, exclaimed—

"By Jove, he *is* thin! I've just been hearing all about the beast from the shikarri; he knows him well. He was a magnificent fellow in his day. The rajah has not the heart to feed him in his old age, and turns him out to pick up a living, or starve—whichever he likes. *He* is not going to pay for his keep, and so the poor brute is dying by inches. Every now and then, when there is a 'tamasha,' he is sent for—for a rajah without elephants is like a society woman without diamonds."

"And the twelve chupatties, and spices, and sugar?" I exclaimed.

"All moonshine!" was the laconic reply.

I thought a great deal of that miserable famishing animal. He preyed on my mind, in the watches of the night: I could hear him through the open window, moving restlessly among the bushes. I was sorely tempted to rise and steal my own loaves, and give him every crumb in the larder!

Next morning I boldly commanded four enormous cakes to be made, and took them to him myself. He seemed to know me, and swallowed them down with wolfish avidity.

When we were fishing that same evening I noticed the elephant down in the shallows of the river, standing knee-deep in the rushes; his figure, in profile against the orange sunset, looked exactly like the arch of a bridge, so wasted was he.

In the course of a day or two we had firmly cemented our acquaintance. Shere Bahadur came up to the verandah for sugar-cane and bread, and salaamed to me ostentatiously whenever we met.

"As we are feeding the beast, we may as well make use of him," remarked Tom, one morning. "The mahout declares that the rajah will let us have him for his keep, and his own wages—six rupees a month. We can have a howdah, and the elephant will be very useful when we get among the long grass and the deer."

"Yes, do let us have him," I gladly agreed. I could not endure to leave him behind, to return to his ration of neem leaves and semi-starvation. Tom therefore despatched a "chit" by the mahout to the rajah, and the next day Shere Bahadur came shuffling back, carrying a howdah and his owner's sanction, also a paper which Tom was requested to sign.

This document (written on the leaf of a copy-book, in English, with immense flourishes) set forth—"That Tom would guarantee to hand Shere Bahadur back, in good condition, at the end of two months, and that if anything happened to the elephant, short of natural death, Tom was responsible for the value of the animal, and the sum of two thousand rupees."

"Well," said Tom, "it is fair enough, though I doubt if the poor old bag of bones is worth two hundred rupees. He will be well fed, and returned in good case, and if he dies now on our hands, after living a century, it will be a base piece of ingratitude for all your kindness; however, there is life in the old boy yet. You and he are great chums. He is a splendid shikar elephant, though a bit slow. I think it is a capital bunderbast." And he signed.

The mahout (now our servant) was full of zeal and zest, and came and laid his head on my feet, and assured me that "I was his father and his mother, and that he was my slave."

I took care to see Shere Bahadur fed daily. He now really received a dozen thick chupatties, and plenty of sugar-cane and ghoor, and his expression lost its look of anguish and famine, though it was early days to expect any improvement in his figure. When we marched, he accompanied us, and I rode in the howdah and enjoyed it. He picked his way so cleverly, and thrust branches aside from our path so carefully, and seemed (though this may be a wild flight of imagination) to *like* to work for me. He was capital at going through jungle, or over rough ground, but in marshy places the poor dear old gentleman seemed to have great difficulty in getting along, and to have but little power in his hind quarters.

Six weeks of our leave had melted away, as it were—time had passed but too rapidly. Shere Bahadur proved invaluable out shooting. Thanks to him, Tom had got a fine tigress, and Charlie some splendid head of deer. They looked so odd in the high elephant grass—no elephant to be seen, but merely two men, as it were sailing along in a howdah. Our last days were, alas! drawing near; our stores were becoming perilously low. It was the end of March, the grass and leaves were dry as tinder and brittle as glass, as the hot winds swept over them. Yes, it was imperative to exchange these charming tents for the thick cat-haunted thatch of our commonplace bungalow. We were all sunburnt, happy, and somewhat shabby. I had contrived to see something of India, after all. I knew the habits of some of the birds and beasts—the names of flowers and trees. I had gazed at my own reflection in lonely forest pools, that were half covered with water-lilies, and from whose sedgy margin flocks of bright-plumaged water-fowl had flashed.

I had met the peacock and his wives leisurely sauntering home after a night of pillage in the grain fields. I had seen, in a sunny glade, a wild dog playing with her puppies. I had watched the big rohu turning lazily over in the river; the sly grey alligator lying log-like on the bank; the blue-bull, or nilgai, dashing through the undergrowth. In short, I had seen a good deal, though I *was* dull.

Twice a day I visited my dear friend Shere Bahadur. I had become quite attached to him, and I firmly believe that he loved me devotedly. One evening I arrived rather earlier than usual on my rounds, and discovered the mahout in deep converse with another man, a stranger, who brought his visit to an abrupt close, and said, as he hurried away, "Teen Roze" (*i.e.* "three days"), to which the mahout responded, "Bahout Atcha" (*i.e.* "good").

"It is my Bhai," he explained. Every one seems to be every one else's brother, especially suspicious-looking acquaintances. "He has come a long journey with a message from my father—my father plenty sick, calling for me." An every-day excuse for "taking leave," only second to the death of the delinquent's grandmother.

On the afternoon of the third day we found it too hot to go out early, and were sitting in our dining-room tent fanning ourselves vigorously and playing "spoof," when we suddenly heard a great commotion—a sound of shouting and running and trumpeting. A tiger, or a "must" elephant, was my first idea. Yes, there it was! A cry of "The elephant! the elephant!" It was an elephant—*my* elephant. We hurried to where a crowd of all our retainers had collected. A quarter of a mile away there was a sudden dip in the ground, a half-dried-up pool of water, covered with a glaze of dark blue scum, surrounded by an expanse of black oozy mud, fringed with rushes and great water-reeds,—the sort of place that was the sure haunt of malarious fever—and struggling in the midst of the quagmire was Shere Bahadur. He had already sunk up to his shoulders, whilst his mahout lay on the bank tearing his hair, beating his head upon the ground, and shrieking at intervals, "My life is departing! my life is departing!" Tom angrily ordered him to arise, and get to his place on the animal's back, and endeavour to guide him out at the safest part; but it appeared to be all quagmire, and quivered for yards at every movement of the elephant. The mahout gibbered, and sobbed, but complied. He scrambled on to Shere Bahadur's neck, and yelled, gesticulated, urged, and goaded. No need; the poor brute was aware of the danger—he was labouring now, not for other people's profit or pleasure, but for his own life. Every one ran for wood, wine-cases, or branches, and flung them to the elephant; and it was pitiful to see how eagerly he snatched at them, and placed them beneath him, and endeavoured to build himself a foothold. After long and truly desperate exertions, he got his forelegs right up on the sound ground, ropes were thrown to him, but, alas! it was all of no avail; the morass was a peculiarly bad one, and his powerless hind quarters were unable to complete the effort and land him safely. No, the cruel quagmire slowly, surely, and remorselessly sucked him down; and, after a most determined effort on the part of the spectators, and a frenzied but impotent struggle on his own, Tom turned to me and exclaimed—

"Poor old boy! it's not a bit of good; he will have to go!"

"Go where?" I cried. "He can be saved; he must be saved," I added, hysterically.

"Impossible; he has not sufficient power to raise himself; the ground is a sort of quicksand. If there was another elephant here, we might manage to haul him out; but, as it is, it is a mere question of time—he will be gone in half an hour."

I wept, implored, ran about like one demented, begging, bribing, entreating the natives to help. And, I must confess, they all did their very best, nobly led by Tom and Charlie. But their efforts were fruitless. Shere Bahadur's hour had come. He had escaped bullets, grape-shot, and tiger, to be gradually swallowed down by that slimy black quagmire, and—horrible thought—buried alive! At the end of a quarter of an hour he had sunk up to his ears, and had ceased to struggle. His trunk was still above the mud. His poor hidden sides!—we could hear them going like the paddle-wheels of a steamer. It appeared to me that his eye sought mine!

Oh, I could endure the scene no longer. I left the crowd to see the very end, rushed back to the tent, flung myself on my bed, covered up my head, and wept myself nearly blind. It seemed hours and hours—twenty-four hours—before Tom came in, and said, as solemnly as if he were announcing the death of a friend, "It is all over."

* * * * *

The detestable mahout over-acted his part; at first he simulated frenzy, his grief far surpassed mine, he gibbered, wept, and beat his breast, and rolled upon the ground at our feet in a paroxysm of anguish, as he assured us that the rajah was a ruthless lord, and that when he returned to Betwa without the Hathi he would certainly be put to torture, and subsequently to death. And then Tom suddenly bethought himself of the terms of the agreement. The elephant had *not* died a natural death. No, he had "gone down quick into the pit." He was dead, and Tom was bound to pay two thousand rupees (about £150). He looked exceedingly glum, but there was no other alternative; yes, he must pay—even if he could not contrive to look pleasant. He most reluctantly sent the rajah a cheque for the amount on the Bank of Bengal, and the mahout departed with somewhat suspicious alacrity, leaving the howdah behind him.

Afterwards, we became acquainted with two extraordinary facts. One was that the rajah had carefully arranged for the death of the elephant, even before we left our first camp; that the mahout's so-called brother was simply a special messenger, who had been despatched to "hurry up" the tragedy. Discovery the second, that the mahout had been seen by our shikarri and several other men deliberately goading and urging the elephant into the quagmire. The wise animal had at first steadily resisted, but putting implicit faith in his rider—who had driven him for years—and being the most docile of his race, he had ultimately yielded, and obediently waded in to his death. At first we indignantly refused to credit these stories, and declared that they were merely the ordinary malicious native slander; but subsequently a slip of copy-book paper was discovered in the pocket of the howdah, which, being interpreted by Tom, read as follows—

"Make no delay. Bad quagmire. Give fifty rupees.—Betwa."

And Shere Bahadur was betrayed for that sum.

We received in due time an effusive letter from the Rajah of Betwa, written, as usual, on the leaf of a copy-book, and inscribed with numerous ornamental flourishes. He also enclosed a formal stamped receipt, which is on my bill-file at the present moment, and is not the least remarkable of the many curious documents there impaled. It says—

"Received from Mister Captain Thomas Hay, the sum of two thousand government rupees, the value of one War elephant—lost!"

"Proven or Not Proven?"

The True Story of Naim Sing, Rajpoot.

Look around, and above, with your mind's eye, and behold high hills and deep narrow valleys—valleys overflowing with corn, and hills speckled with flocks; no, these are not the Alps,—nor yet the Andes; the sturdy brown people have the Tartar type of face, their stubborn, shaggy ponies are of Thibetan breed. You stand on the borders of Nepaul, and among the lower slopes of the great Himalayas—a remote district, but tolerably populated and prosperous. There are many snug, flat-roofed houses scattered up and down the niches in these staircase-like heights, encompassed with cowsheds, melon gardens, groves of walnut trees, and a few almost perpendicular acres of murga (grain); their proprietors are well-to-do, their wants inconsiderable, the possession of a pony, half a dozen goats, and a couple of milch buffaloes, constitutes a man of means, who is as happy in his way as, perhaps happier than, the English or Irish owner of a great landed estate. Moreover, this pastoral life has its pleasures: there are holy festivals, fairs, feasts, wrestling-matches,—and occasionally a little gambling and cock-fighting. But even in these primitive mountain regions, life is not *all* Arcadian simplicity; there are black spots on the sun of its existence, such as envy, hatred, malice, jealousy, false-witness, and murder.

Peaceful, even to sleepiness, as the district appears, serene and immovable as the grand outline of its lofty white horizon, nevertheless this remote corner of the world has been the scene of a renowned trial—a trial which outrivalled many a notorious case in far-away Europe for exciting violent disputes, disturbances, and bloodshed—a trial which convulsed Kumaon, Kali Kumaon, and Gurwalh—whose effects, as it were the ripples from a stone cast into still waters, are experienced to the present hour in the shape of curses, collisions, and feuds. At the root of the trouble was, as usual, a woman.

Durali (which signifies 'darling') was the grandchild and only surviving relative of Ahmed Dutt, a thriftless, shrivelled old hill-man, who smoked serrus (or Indian hemp) until he brought himself into a condition of imbecility, and suffered his worldly affairs to go to ruin; his hungry cattle and goats strayed over his neighbours' lands, he cared not for crops, nor yet for wor-hos (boundary marks), he cared for nought but his huka, and his warm padded quilt, and abandoned the beautiful Durali, like the cattle, to her own devices. Now, according to Durali, these devices were supremely innocent: she spun wool, kept fowl, laboured somewhat fitfully in the fields, and tended the jungle of dahlias and marigolds which threatened to swallow up the little slab-roofed dwelling—that was all. So said Ahmed Dutt's granddaughter, but public opinion held a different view; it lifted up its voice (in a shrill treble), and declared that Durali, being by general consent the most beautiful woman in Kumaon, had wrung the hearts of half the young—ay, and old—men in the province; that of a truth her suitors were legion; but that she turned her back on all of them—as she would have fools to believe—no!

Her grandfather was indigent, as who could deny? Whence, then, the rich silver necklet, the bangles, the great belt of uncut turquoise, blue as the spring sky—whence the strong Bhootia pony? Had Ahmed Dutt been otherwise than a smoke-sodden idiot and a dotard, he had, according to custom, sold this valuable chattel a full year ago, and received as her price three hundred rupees, yea, and young asses, perchance, and buffaloes. As it was, Durali ruled him tyrannically, flouted all humble pretenders for her hand, and at eighteen years of age was her own mistress, fancy-free, poor, ambitious, and beautiful—miraculously beautiful! since her wondrous loveliness stirred even the leathern hearts of these hill-men; and she possessed a face, figure, craft, and coquetry, amply warranted to set the whole of Kumaon in a blaze. Yea, the saying that "to be her friend was unfortunate, to be her suitor beckoned death," deterred but few. It was undeniable that Farid Khan had fallen over the khud, on the bad road to Pura; do not his bones lie, to this day, unburied and bleaching, at the foot of that awful precipice? *Who* said that his rival, Jye Bhan, had pushed him in the dark? Who could prove it? At any rate, he was no more. As was also Kalio Thapa, carried away by a mighty flood in the Sardah river—how it befell, who could say? And there was, moreover, Phulia, who had certainly hanged himself because Durali had spurned him.

Many were her adorers, and exceedingly bitter the hatred they bore to one another.

Durali was tall, erect, and Juno-like, with a skin like new wheat, features of a bold Greek type, abundant jet-black hair, and a pair of magnificent eyes. Other women declared that there was magic in these—certainly they spoke with tongues, they commanded, exhorted, entreated, dazzled, and bewitched.

But Durali owed nothing to the fine feathers which enhance the attractions of so many fine birds. She wore a dark-blue petticoat and short cotton jacket, a few bangles and a copper charm—the ordinary attire of an ordinary Pahari girl; dress could add but little to her superb personality.

The handsome granddaughter of Ahmed Dutt was well known by reputation in the surrounding villages, her name was in every one's mouth, her fame had penetrated even as far as Almora itself. At the sacred feast of the Dusserah, where crowds assemble to behold the yearly sacrifice, there Durali appeared for the first time, and in gala costume, wearing a short-sleeved red velveteen bodice, an enviable silver necklet, and a flower behind each ear. The eyes of half the multitude were riveted on the hill beauty—instead of the devoted buffalo, which had been tied up for days, at the quarter guard of the Ghoorkas, and now innocently awaited its impending fate.

Yes, people actually thronged, and pressed, and pushed, and strove, in order to obtain a good look at the famous Durali, for whom men had contended, and fought—ay, and died.

* * * * *

There was a sudden lull in the loud hum of voluble Pahari tongues, and all attention was concentrated on a renowned athlete, who stepped forward with the huge Nepaulese sacrificial knife in his hand, and with one swift dexterous blow severed the buffalo's ponderous head from his body. Immediately ensued a frenzied rush on the part of the spectators, in order to dip a piece of cloth in the smoking blood. There was also a determined, nay, a ferocious struggle between two young men, as to which should have the privilege of plunging Durali's handkerchief, on her behalf, into the holy stream. This coveted office fell to Naim Sing, who wrung the cloth from the feebler grasp of Johar, the son of Turroo. This contest over a blood-stained rag was noted at the time. It was an evil omen, and more than one old crone shook her grey head, as she muttered, "Mark ye, my sisters, there will be yet more trouble between the strivers—yea, bloodshed."

The victor was the son of Bhowan Sing, who lived in the village of Beebadak, and cultivated a considerable amount of fertile land. He had three sons—Umed Sing, Rattan Sing, and Naim Sing; the latter was the Benjamin of the family, a handsome youth, with a lithe, symmetrical figure, bold eloquent grey eyes, and crisp black locks, the champion wrestler of his pergunnah (and of the district); possessed not merely of an active and powerful body, but an active and powerful mind. His appearance, his age, and his stronger character, were not the only reasons that made him looked up to by his brethren and neighbours, and a ruler in his father's house; some two years previously, whilst digging a well, he had discovered a pot of coins, and was now the owner of twenty pairs of pearls, fifty gold mohurs, four ponies, and a herd of milch buffaloes. Happy the woman whom Naim Sing would take to wife!

Johar, the son of Turroo, was a sturdy, square-faced youth, honest and cheerful, who had nought to cast into the balance against prowess, ponies, and pearls, save one slender accomplishment, and his heart—he played somewhat skilfully on a whistle, which was fashioned out of the thigh-bone of a man, and profusely studded with great rough turquoises. He was in much request at all the revellings within thirty miles—that is to say, Johar with his whistle.

Not long after the Dusserah, the venerable Ahmed Dutt smoked himself peacefully out of this world, and was duly burnt, with every necessary formality. His granddaughter being left forlorn, now took an old woman to live with her in the little stone house under the edge of the Almora road, as you go to Loher Ghât. Durali was in straitened circumstances; the murga crop had failed, three of her lean kine were dead, but she was befriended by Naim Sing, who evinced much sympathy for her desolate condition; and it was a matter of whispered gossip that Johar was also secretly performing acts of kindness—secretly, indeed, for none dared to put themselves into competition with the formidable Naim Sing,—and it was believed that he was the favoured suitor.

At harvest-time, Naim Sing was compelled to be absent for ten days, on an urgent mission to the foot of the hills. Immediately on his return, he hastened to Durali's hut, and found her absent. Wearied by a rapid march of thirty miles, he cast himself down among the long rice stalks at the foot of a choora tree, and there impatiently awaited the reappearance of his divinity. As he lay half dozing in the heat, his practised ear heard steps and voices, and looking through the rice stalks he beheld a couple leisurely approaching. The man was playing on a bone whistle, and the woman carried sheaves of wheat upon her stately head. There was no difficulty in recognizing Durali and Johar. The jealous watcher lay still, listening eagerly with quick-coming breath. It appeared to him that the beguiling Durali by no means discouraged her companion's advances, which were couched in the usual flowery terms of Oriental flattery. "Oh, woman, thou hast sheaves on thy head, but they appear like clusters of pomegranates on thy shoulders. There is none like thee. The light of thy beauty hath illumined my soul! As for Naim Sing, he is a seller of dog's flesh! an owl, the son of an owl; he is vain as the sandpiper, who sleeps with his legs up, in order to support the sky at night. Listen, O core of my heart! it hath come to mine ears, that trade and barter have nought to do with his hasty excursions to the plains—he hath a wife at Huldwani—hence his journeys."

This was too much for the endurance of his enraged listener, who, leaping furiously upon Johar, clove his head with his heavy tulwar (sword). Johar staggered, blinded with blood, and defenceless, then, turning, ran for his life; but his infuriated enemy, flinging the shrieking girl to one side, swiftly pursued the wounded wretch to where he had sought refuge in a cowshed, dashed in the frail door, and there despatched him. Presently he returned, fierce-eyed, savage, blood-stained, to confront the horror-stricken and trembling Durali.

"Woman," he cried hoarsely, "I have slain him—thine the sin. His death be on thy head!"

But she, with many tears and vows, vociferously protested her innocence, and in a surprisingly short time appeased Naim Sing's wrath. Now that the rage of his jealousy and vengeance had been satisfied, he began to realize the result of his passion; he had slain a man—not the first who had met his death at his hands. He had once killed an antagonist in a wrestling-match—that was a misadventure; this was—well, the Sirkar would call it—murder.

The shades of evening had not yet fallen, and until then he dared not set about concealing the corpse. He found Durali a cunning adviser and an unscrupulous accomplice. Men die hard, especially wiry hill-men, and Johar had not passed away in silence; his expiring groans were heard by Bucko, the old woman, and Naim Sing was therefore compelled to admit her into the secret.

When the moon rose, the three conspirators bound up the body and carried it down to one of the fields, there they carefully uprooted each stalk, each distinct plant, growing over the surface of what was to form the future grave, which was next excavated, and Johar, the son of Turroo, was dropped into the hole, his whistle flung contemptuously after him, and both were presently covered up with earth—and wheat.

The burying-party returned to the hut, where Naim Sing inflicted a small wound on his leg with a cut of his tulwar, in order to support the statement he proposed making to the authorities, that Johar had attacked him with murderous intent, and, having failed in his effort, fled. Next morning Naim Sing called on the Tehel-seldhar and made his report, and the Tehel-seldhar despatched a tokdar (responsible official for a cluster of villages) to take steps for the capture of Johar, the son of Turroo. But Johar was not to be found, or even heard of, and his own family became seriously alarmed, and suspected foul play. If he had fled and departed on a long journey, wherefore had he left his boots, clothes, and money behind? The connections of Naim Sing were powerful, their pirohet, or family priest, his personal friend—rumour and suspicion were strangled—but there were grave whispers round the fires in the huts, all over the hills: what had befallen Johar, the son of Turroo?

However, a murder was a common event. Blood-feuds were acknowledged, and soon the circumstance was allowed to fade into oblivion by all but Rateeban, a lame man, Johar's twin brother, who took a solemn oath at Gutkoo temple to avenge him. He suspected Durali; he watched her and her house by stealth. Why was one small corner of the wheat-field uncut? He made her overtures of friendship, he flattered, he fawned; by dint of judicious questions, and even more judicious information, Rateeban gained his end. Oh, false love! Oh, treachery! Oh, woman! it was the beautiful Durali who led Rateeban to his brother's grave, who showed him the blood splashes on the cowshed walls, who told him the truth. Yes, jealousy is doubtless as cruel as the grave. Durali had capitulated and given her long-beleaguered heart wholly to Naim Sing—his eloquence, good looks, prowess,—ay, and presents,—had carried the citadel, and lo! the dead man's words were verified. Naim Sing had already a wife at Huldwani, a bold dark woman of the plains, to whom he was secretly wed by strictest and securest ceremonial.

To the amazement and indignation of himself and his kinsmen, Naim Sing was arrested and carried to Almora jail, there to await his trial; his friends and connections (who were many and powerful) made a desperate attempt to secure his release; bribes, and even threats, were used; but what could avail against the evidence of the treacherous Durali?—and the evidence of the dead body? Yes, Naim Sing, the champion wrestler, the leading youth in his district, handsome, popular, rich, in the full zenith of his days and vigour, was bound to be despatched to the dark muggy shores of the Salween river, and end his existence ingloriously in

Moulmein jail. Never again would he take part in a wrestling-match, or breast his native mountains and chase the ibex and makor; his beloved hills, and his ancestral home, would know him no more. Rateeban, Johar's lame brother, would have preferred the blood of his enemy, but was fain to be contented with his sentence, "Transportation for life." He exulted savagely in his revenge, and actually accompanied the gang of wretched prisoners the whole march of ninety miles to the railroad—on foot—in order that he might enjoy the ecstasy of gloating over his foe in chains! Each day at sundown, when the party halted, Rateeban came and stood opposite to Naim Sing, and, leaning on his stick, mocked him. It was rumoured that Rateeban was not the sole voluntary escort, but that a woman, veiled, and riding a stout grey pony, stealthily followed the party afar off! It was Durali, who, when it was too late, was distracted with penitence and anguish. Her remorse was eating away her very heart—but to what avail now?

Huldwani is a large, populous native town on the edge of the Terai, a few miles from the foot of the hills, and here a frantic creature awaited the prisoners, or rather the prisoner Naim Sing. She tore her hair, she beat her head upon the ground, and Naim Sing was not unmoved—no. Then she lifted up her hands and her voice, and cursed with hideous screaming curses "that woman who had wrought this great shame and wickedness—that other woman on the hills!" And the other woman, having heard with her ears and seen with her eyes, turned back and retraced those weary ninety miles, *now* more in anger than in sorrow,—for such is human nature.

In less than twelve months, the news came to the hills that Naim Sing had died in Moulmein prison, the death certificate said of atrophia, but his father and brethren called it a broken heart. "He was ever too wild a bird for a cage," proclaimed his kinsmen and friends; and within a short time he was as completely forgotten as Johar, whom he had slain, and Durali, whom he had deceived, and who had disappeared.

* * * * *

After a lapse of twenty years, two men belonging to the village where Rateeban lived, returned from a pilgrimage, and announced that at the great fair at Hardwar, on the Ganges, they had seen *Naim Sing*—who had saluted them as Brahmins. He had with him three horses, and a woman—his wife—and looked in good health, and prosperous. Rateeban, at first angrily incredulous, finally determined to investigate this matter in person, and once more travelled the wearisome ninety miles which lay between his home and the railway. Though every step was painful, he heeded it not, such is the power of hate! With inexhaustible patience, he followed clue after clue; he searched for nearly three months, and was at last rewarded by success. Back up to the hills, to a distant village in Gurwalh, among the spectators at a great wrestling-match, he tracked and found Naim Sing!—Naim Sing, surprisingly little changed. Where were the signs of convict labour, the marks of irons, and of that life that burns into a man's soul? He looked somewhat older, his temples were bald, but his figure was as upright, his foot as firm, his eye as keen as ever. Rateeban swore to him, with fervour, as an escaped convict, and had him instantly arrested. There was no doubt of his identity; there was the self-inflicted scar on his leg, the bone in his arm which had been broken by wrestling. The criminal was brought back to Almora, in order to be arraigned for unlawful return from transportation, and tried under section 226 of the Indian Penal Code.

The tidings of the resurrection and return of Naim Sing was passed by word of mouth from village to village. His father and brethren, his friends and relations, and those of Johar and Rateeban, and, in short, everybody's friends, flocked into Almora to attend the trial. The case was heard in the court-house, which stands within the old fort; and not only was the court itself crammed to suffocation, but the crowds overflowed the surrounding enclosure, even down the narrow stone steps, and away into the streets. Thousands and thousands were assembled, and as the days went on the interest quickened, and the case became a matter of furious contention between two factions—for and against: the party who declared the culprit was indeed the real, true, and only Naim Sing, and the party who swore that he was *not*. Fierce feuds were engendered, torrents of abuse and angry blows were exchanged,—blood was freely shed.

All Kumaon and Gurwalh had encompassed Almora like an invading army, and Kumaon, Gurwalh, and the respectable Goorka station itself, were in an uproar, and seething like a witches' cauldron.

The prisoner stood up boldly, as befitted the namesake of the lion, and confronted his accusers with a haughty and impassive mien. But surely—surely those keen grey eyes were the eyes of Naim Sing!

"I am not the criminal," he declared. "Who is this Naim Sing—this murderer? and what hath he to do with me? Behold I am Krookia, and my father is Rusool Sing, who lives in the village of Tolee; my star is Jeshta and Ras, and my horoscope is with Gunga Josh, if he be yet alive."

Moreover, he brought witnesses, and the certificate of Naim Sing's death in Moulmein jail.

"The people of the pergunnah, which you aver that you belong to, do not know you," said the Crown prosecutor. "But Rateeban recognized you; how can you explain that?"

"There be two Rateebans," was the glib answer, "and one is mine enemy."

"Strange that Rateeban, the enemy of Naim Sing, is your enemy also."

"I doubt not that the lame dog—may his race be exterminated!—hath many foes. I know him not. He hath been the means of sending one man to prison for life, and now, behold, he would despatch another. It is a vicious ambition. As for the people of my village, lo! many years ago, I found a treasure, and my neighbours quarrelled and beat and robbed me. They have no desire to recall their own black deeds, nor my face. I fled to the plains, where I have taken road contracts for the Sirkar, and prospered."

"Naim Sing also found a treasure," said the advocate. "Does the land in these hills yield so many of these crops?"

"By your honour's favour, I cannot tell. I found one treasure, to my cost. Money is a man-slayer."

Many witnesses recognized or repudiated the prisoner, and there was hard swearing on both sides.

At length a young Baboo from Allahabad was put forward—a keen, intelligent, brisk-looking youth, wearing a velvet cap and patent leather boots, embellished with mother-of-pearl buttons.

"Twenty years ago I dwelt in Bareilly," he said. "There were four of us children, my mother, and my father, who was sick unto death. The jail daroga, who was his kinsman, came to him privily one night, and whispered long. I was awake, being an-hungered, and heard all that was said.

"'Lo! Gunesheb, thou art my kinsman. Thou art poor and sick, thy days are numbered; wouldst thou die a rich man?'

"'Would I die in Paradise?' said my father.

"'A gang of convicts pass here to-morrow, on their way to Calcutta and Moulmein beyond the sea. Wilt thou take the place of one of them? Thou art his size and height; thou hast not long to live, he has a strong young life; and in return for thy miserable body he will give four hundred rupees, ten pairs of pearls, one pair of gold bangles, and three ponies.'

"My father went forth that same hour with the jail daroga, and returned no more. Next day my mother wept sore; yea, even though she had gold bangles on her arms, very solid, and pearls and silver in a cloth; also there were three ponies, strong and fat, in our yard. Later, she took us to see when the convicts passed along the road, and we rode on the ponies beside them for two days. She told the warders she had a brother, falsely accused, who was in the gang. He wore a square cap pulled far over his eyes, and he coughed as he marched. As we left, he embraced me tenderly, by favour of the warders. I knew he was my father. Afterwards we went south, and returned to Bareilly no more."

Thus Gunesheb had bartered away his few remaining months of life for the benefit of his family, and Naim Sing had spread a bold free wing, and enjoyed his liberty for twenty years! He had the ceaseless craving of a born hill-man to return to the mountains. The line of snows edging the burnt-up plains had drawn him like a magnet. Slowly but surely, becoming reckless with time and impunity, he had cast fear and caution to the winds, as once more the smell of the pine-needles and of the wood smoke crept into his blood!

As he sat in the dock, the prisoner deliberately scanned every face with an air of lofty indifference. He swore to the last that "he was Krookia, the son of Rusool Sing," but no respectable land-owner identified him under that name. Moreover, the wife of Naim Sing had been recognized at her native place wearing her rings and bangles, sure and certain token that her husband was *alive*; and in the face of overwhelming evidence, the culprit was sentenced for the second time on the same spot to be transported beyond the seas for the term of his natural life.

Then Naim Sing arose, tall and erect, a dignified and impressive figure, carrying his two-score years with grace, and made a most powerful and thrilling appeal in his own defence—an appeal for an innocent man, who was about to be banished for ever from his home and country, because, forsooth, his features had the ill fortune to resemble those of a dead murderer!

During his speech, one could almost hear a leaf fall outside the court. The previous quiet had now changed to what resembled a hush of awe. The audience within and without—the windows and doors stood wide, and exhibited an immense sea of human heads—hung with avidity on each sonorous syllable. Not a gesture, not a glance was lost. So stirring and impassioned was his eloquence, that every heart was shaken, and many were moved to tears. But the condemned man pleaded his cause in vain; in fact, his silver tongue afforded but yet another proof of his identity. His fate was sealed. Fearing a public tumult, he was removed secretly ere dawn, marched down the mountain sides for the last time, despatched to the Andamans,—and there he died.

So ended a trial that lasted many days, that was more discussed and fought over than any law-suit of the period; a case which is fiercely argued and hotly debated even to the present hour; a cause which has divided scores of households and separated chief friends. For there are some who declare that the real Naim Sing expired in Moulmein jail khana nineteen years previously, and that the vengeance of Rateeban demanded two lives for one; also that the heavily bribed son of Gunesheb had borne black false witness, his father having died in his own house; and that, of a truth, an innocent man was condemned to transportation and death: but there be some who think otherwise.

An Outcast of the People.

"Pushed by a power we see not, and struck by a hand unknown,
We pray to the trees for shelter, and press our lips to a stone."

SIR A. LYALL.

Jasoda was seventeen years of age, and fair as a sunrise on the snows. She dwelt in a district not far from the Goomptee river, among the wheat and poppy fields that are scattered over Rohilcund.

As a little girl, all had gone well with her; she was petted and caressed; she played daily in the sun with other village children, erecting palaces and temples with dust and blossoms; her hair was carefully plaited and plastered with cocoanut oil; she wore a big nose-ring, anklets, and bangles—not brass or pewter, but real silver ones, for she was married to the heir of a rich thakur, a delicate, puny boy of her own age. But one rains he died, and there was sore, sore lamentation. Had Jasoda realized what his death signified to her, she would have wailed ten times louder than any paid mourner; but ignorance was surely bliss, and she was not *very* sorry, for Sapona had been greedy, fretful, and tyrannical. He had often struck her, pinched her, and pulled her long plaits, or run screaming with tales to his mother—a fat woman with a shrill tongue and a heavy arm—whom Jasoda feared.

But after Sapona had been carried away to the burning ghâut, all seemed changed; every one appeared to hate Jasoda, yea, even her own grandmother. Her ornaments were taken off, her head was shorn, her cloth, though white, was coarse and old; there were no more games under the tamarind trees, and no more sweets. Jasoda's life was blighted in the bud, for, at the tender age of six, she was that miserable outcast, a Braminee widow. Poor pariah! she would stand aloof, with wide-open wistful eyes (ostentatiously shunned by the other children in the courtyard), and wonder what it all meant. She would piteously inquire of her grandmother, as the crone sat spinning cotton, "What she had done. Wherefore might she not eat with her, and why did Jooplee push her, and strike her, if she approached her? and wherefore did her mother-in-law, and other women, hold aside their clothes lest she should touch them as she passed?"

"The shadow of a widow is to be dreaded, and—it is the custom, it is our religion," muttered the old woman, as if speaking to herself. No doubt the days of suttee were better; then the girl had one grand hour, applauded by the world; she was holy and sanctified, and hers was a glorious triumph as she walked in procession behind the tom-toms, whilst thousands looked on with awe, and the devout pressed forward to touch her garments. Was not a moment like that worth years of drudgery and misery, blows and scorn? True, at the end of the march, there was the funeral pyre under the peepul tree; but if there was oil among the faggots, and the wood was not too green, and the priests plied the suttee with sufficient bhang, it was nought! And her screams were always drowned in the shouting and the tom-toms. She herself had seen a suttee; yes, and the girl was forced into it. She had no spirit; she wept, and shrieked, and struggled,—so people had whispered,—but her relations drove her to the faggots, for the family of a suttee are held in much esteem! Truly it were better for Jasoda, this child with the beautiful face, to have died for the honour of her people than to live to be their scapegoat and their slave!

As years went on, and hot weather, monsoon, and cold season passed, and crops were sown and cut, and there were births and marriages and deaths, Jasoda grew up. She was now seventeen, and very fair to see. Her mother-in-law hated her, as did also her brother; and, more than all, her brother's wife, and her sisters-in-law. In spite of their fine silk sarees and gold ornaments, they were but little stars, whilst this accursed girl was as the sun at noonday!

Jasoda was the drudge of the family,—a large clan, dwelling, as is customary, within the same enclosure. These courtyards, built irregularly, somewhat resemble a child's house of cards; narrow footpaths between the mud walls compose the village streets. You may steer your way among these beaten tracks, and beneath these sun-baked entrenchments, and never see a single house; merely various postern doors which enclose a space, possibly containing ten hovels, and as many families. One of the largest courtyards in the village belonged to Padooram, the brother of Jasoda; he was the richest man in the whole pergunnah, owned land and cattle and plough bullocks, and had no bunnia's claims to disquiet his sleep. His wife, a fat, pock-marked woman, boasted real gold bangles, and a jewelled nose-ring, and was the envy of her sex. There was Jasoda's father and mother-in-law, and Monnee and Puthao, their married daughters; her younger brother; his wife and family; also her old grandmother; and Jasoda was the servant of them all. Truly they were hard masters and merciless mistresses. She, their slave, arose at dawn. She drew water till her arms ached. She ground meal, and cooked, and polished the brass cooking-vessels; she carried the clothes of these households to the ghât, and washed them; she minded the children, and milked the buffaloes, and herded the cattle. More than this, when one of the plough bullocks was sick, her brother placed the yoke on Jasoda's shoulders, and drove her as companion to the spotted ox, up and down the long furrows, and in the sight of all people. To them it was as nought; no one cried shame, or pitied her—she was only a *widow*. In the harvest season there was much to do, from daylight till dusk, cutting cane and corn, and carrying and stacking, and working at the sugar-press. Sometimes, strong girl as she was, Jasoda wept from sheer weariness. Yet, for all this toil, she barely got enough to keep her from semi-starvation. She was flung the scraps that were left from meals, as well as the rags of the family. Nor did she ever receive one kind word or look, not even from her grandmother. However, she was amply compensated for this cruel indifference from another source. Many were the kind words and looks bestowed on her by the young men of the village; but Jasoda was proud. Jooplee, her sister-in-law, famed for the most evil mind and wicked tongue within many koss, even *she* could find no cause of offence in her drudge, save that she was the fairest maiden in all the taluka, and this fault she punished with the zeal and vigour of an envious and ugly woman! Jasoda was desperately unhappy. What had she done to men or gods, to be treated thus cruelly? And there was nothing to look forward to, even in twenty years' time. Her present lot would only be altered by death—and after death? There was no future existence for such as *she*. Many a time she crept away, and poured out all her wrongs to the squat stone idol daubed with red paint, whose temple was the shade of the peepul tree. She asked him, "Why women were ever born into the land?" and besought his help with tears and passionate pleadings. In vain she cried, "Ram, ram," and took him offerings of flowers, and gashed her arm with a sickle, and shed her hot young blood before him. He maintained his habitual placid pose, his vacant stare, his graven grin, and gave no sign. No, at the end of six weary moons there was still no answer to her prayers. Heart-sick, Jasoda now went and gazed longingly at the river. She stole away to visit it whilst her relations took their midday rest in the cane-fields. Alas! it was very low, and fat muggers lay upon its grey mud banks, as lazy as so many logs of wood, though their evil little eyes were active enough—watching for floating corpses. No, no; a big rapid torrent in the rains, with a strong flood, fed by the far-away snows, rushing boldly onward, bearing great blocks of foam on its brown bosom,—into *that* she could cast herself, but not into one of these slow, slimy channels, creeping past greasy banks, whereon ravenous alligators would battle for her body.

As time advanced, the tyranny of the family became more oppressive, and Jasoda threw patience to the winds—indeed, it had long been threadbare. To be sent five or six koss in the burning June sun, to gratify the momentary whim of Taramonnee, a child, or, rather, imp of five, was beyond endurance, and represented the proverbial "last straw." The domestic martyr being hopeless and desperate, now turned on her tormentors, as a leopardess at bay. Why should she be as an ox, a beast of burthen, all her days? She gave shrill invective for invective, accepted curses and blows with sullen indifference, and refused to work beyond a certain portion. Yea, they might kill her, if they so willed; it would be all the better; and she oscillated between fits of hot passion and moods of cold obstinacy. Her aged grandmother could not imagine what had happened to the household slave. She was usually so long-suffering, so easily driven and abused. The hag and the other women put their heads together and took counsel, whilst the rebel sat aloof in a dark corner of her hut, like some wild animal in its den, her fixed dark eyes staring out on the glaring white courtyard with an expression of intense, hopeless despair. She hated every one. She felt that she could almost kill them. Truly she had been born in an evil hour and under an evil star, and she cursed both hour and planet. There were Junia and Talloo, girls who had played with her: each had a husband and babies and bangles; yea, and cows of their own. Why was she beaten and half starved, and treated like a stray pariah dog? She was handsomer than either. Isa, the son of Ganga, had told her that her eyes were stars, her teeth as seed pearls, and her lips like the bud of the pomegranate; yet these fat, ugly women slept at ease on their charpoys, whilst she toiled in the cold grey dawn or in the scorching noonday heat!

Above all creatures who breathed, she detested Jooplee, her sister-in-law, the mother of Taramonnee; and next to her, Taramonnee, a shrill-voiced, malignant imp, who pinched and bit her secretly, and who once—when she was tied up and beaten—danced before her, and made mouths at her and mocked her, clapping her hands with fiendish ecstasy.

For many months a great fire had been smouldering in Jasoda's heart, and woe be to the hand that stirred it! Once more it was the cane-cutting season, and she was toiling hard all day, reaping and carrying and stacking. She was very very weary, and whilst the carts lumbered villagewards with the last load, she sat down under a peepul tree to rest. It was the soft hour of sunset, the cattle were going home, bats were flickering to and fro, the low evening smoke lay like a pale blue veil over the land: smoke from fires where many hungry people were baking the universal chupatti. Jasoda fell fast asleep, and dreamt. Her dreams were pleasant, for she dreamt that she was dead. Suddenly she was rudely awoke by an agonizing pain. No, it was not a snake-bite; it was a pinch from the sharp strong fingers of Jooplee's daughter, who, gazing intently into her face, cried with malicious glee—

"Ah, lazy one, arise and work! I shall tell of thee, and to-night thou shalt be beaten. The neighbours refuse to believe that father beats thee, because thou dost not scream. Mother said so. But thou shalt scream to-night, so that thy cries can be heard as far as the bunnia's shop. Get up, pig!" And she pushed her with her foot.

It needed but a touch like this to rouse the sleeping flame. Instantly Jasoda sprang erect, rage in her heart and murder in her eye. At least she would rid herself of this insect, and, snatching up a stone, she dashed it at the child with all the force of a muscular arm, and with the fury of years of repressed passion. The aim was true, and Taramonnee fell. For a second her limbs twitched convulsively, and then she lay still—oh, tragically still.

"Rise!" screamed Jasoda. "Rise! and may thine eyes be darkened, thou little devil!"

But there was no movement; Taramonnee was evidently stunned. Jasoda stooped and raised her, whilst a terrible fear crept over her. The child's head fell back, her hand dropped. Was it possible? Could she be *dead*? Yes, she was dead, though she had not meant to kill her; and, since she could not bring her to life, what was she to do? She gazed with horror at this awful, motionless thing, whose life she herself had taken, oh, how easily! She could no longer endure those staring, glazing eyes, she must put them out of her sight. Raising the limp body with a supreme effort, she carried it in her arms to a dry well at some distance, and then averting her face, she threw it down. It struck against the sides, with a dull muffled sound, and fell to the bottom with a hideous crash that made her shudder. As Jasoda went slowly homewards, she was conscious that she was now the same as Moola, the son of Maldhu, who had cut his wife's throat with a sickle; or the city girl, who drowned her baby in the tank in the Mango tope. She cooked the evening meal as usual, and heard Jooplee inquire for Taramonnee, and send to seek her at a neighbour's; presently she became anxious, talked of snakes, hyenas, and devils, and even went herself to each postern door, and called, "Taramonnee, Taramonnee;" but she never once thought of inquiring about her from the sullen girl who was washing the cooking-pots. The old grandmother said soothingly, "Surely she hath gone with Almonee, who lives across the river." But this did not satisfy her anxious parent, and the neighbourhood was summoned, and a great search made. It was full moon—a splendid harvest moon—and bright as day. All night long Jasoda lay awake, watching the moonbeams and listening to the melancholy howl of the jackals, and the heavy thud of the ripe banka fruit as it fell in the courtyard. Should she run away or stay? she asked herself. She debated the vital question long, and finally resolved that she would abide and await her fate! She was weary of life. Why prolong it? The river was low; best perish by the rope, and thus end all. At least she would have rest and peace, and perhaps a new and better life in another world.

At daybreak, the body of Taramonnee was brought in and laid before her mother, who tore her hair in a frenzy, and beat her head against the wall. The hakim was summoned, and solemnly declared that the child had not met her death by accident. No; behold, there was the blow on her temple; of a surety, she had been murdered,—and by whom? Jooplee read the answer in Jasoda's eyes.

"Yes, I struck her," admitted the girl boldly. "She came to me by the cane-field, and pinched me sorely when I was asleep. I am *glad* she is dead."

She repeated the same story to four police, who arrived at noon, and bound her arms, and led her away to jail. She suffered it to be believed that she had murdered the child in cold blood, and thrown her down the well. Jasoda's case was unusually simple; there was but a brief trial. The culprit offered no defence, and had apparently no friends. It was known that she had always hated Taramonnee and her mother; she had found the former alone, had slain her,—and was glad. Her own mouth destroyed her. The village was in a ferment. The court was crowded; Jooplee and her people were ravening for revenge. As for Jasoda's kindred, they knew she must be hanged—which thing was worse than suttee—disgrace instead of glory would cover them! When asked if she had aught to say, Jasoda stood up before the judge, a beautiful young creature, with the passionate dark eyes and the regular features of her race, and the form of a Grecian nymph, and answered distinctly—

"No, my lord sahib, I care not for my life; and, if it is the will of the sirkar, let them take it." To herself she said, "Better this end than the other; the river is low."

As Jasoda lay under sentence of death, her venerable grandmother bestirred herself to save her. She was a shrivelled, hideous old hag, with a ragged red chuddah over her head, and she sat at the gate of the judge's compound daily, and cried for the space of two hours without ceasing.

"Do hai! Do hai! Do hai!" *i.e.* "Mercy! mercy! mercy!" She then adjourned to the cantonment magistrate's abode, and shrieked the same prayer outside his gates; and finally to the civil surgeon's, who was also the jail superintendent; and to him, for this reason, she devoted one hour extra, and her voice never once failed. Thus much for being the scold of the village! There was intense excitement in the neighbourhood as the day of execution drew nigh, and lo! one evening, when a great gallows was raised on the maidan, there were already collected thousands of people, precisely as if it were some holy spot, a scene of pilgrimage—all attracted by the same desire—to see a woman hanged!

It was indeed a grand tamasha. The crowds far surpassed in numbers those who assembled at the yearly feast. The local inhabitants noted with complacency the hundreds of total strangers who came for many miles on foot, on ponies, or in ekkas. Old Sona ceased now to scream and beat her breast. She felt like one of the actors in a tremendous tragedy, and was the object of a certain amount of curiosity and attention—a position that was entirely novel, and—alas! alas! that it must be chronicled—secretly enjoyed. The sun rose on the fatal day—the last sunrise Jasoda would ever see—the great prison gates opened, and a body of police marched slowly forth. Then came Jasoda, walking between two warders. There was a murmur among the throng. She was surprisingly fair to behold, and for once in her life she wore a dress like girls of her class. A wealthy and eccentric woman in the city had sent it to her. Yes, she was as fair as the newly risen dawn. She stood and steadily surveyed the immense expectant multitude. She recognized the eyes of many people from her own village fixed upon her with a mixture of interest and awe. She beheld her old grandmother, and her brother, and Moonee, and Pathoo, and Jai Singh, the son of Herk Singh, who had compared her to Parbutti herself and to the new moon. It seemed to her that to be the centre of interest to so vast a throng was almost as fine as a suttee! The last moment arrived, and the superintendent asked her if she had anything to say, any bequests to make.

"Bequests!" and she almost laughed. "Truly I have nothing in the world save a few rags. But thou mayest give my body to my grandmother; she seems sorry. I have nothing to say. The child hurt me, and I struck her. I meant not to kill her; nevertheless, she died; that is all. She is dead, and I shall soon be dead also."

Jasoda's fortitude did not fail her—no, not when her arms were pinioned, her petticoats tied about her feet, the cap drawn over her face. She never once quailed or trembled.

* * * * *

When the body had been cut down, and the crowd had dispersed, the superintendent sent for the old grandmother, who came, dry-eyed and fierce.

"It is somewhat against rules," he said, "but I am going to grant you the girl's only request: she said you were to have her body—take it away, and burn it!"

"I!" shrieked the harridan. "*I* touch her after the dones (hangmen) have laid their hands on her! *I*, a high-caste Braminee! Do with the carrion as thou wilt!" and she spat on the ground and went her way. Thus, after death, neglect and scorn pursued poor hot-tempered Jasoda, even to the grave.

Nevertheless, had she but known it, her wrongs were most amply avenged. Who was there to do the work of the family—nay, of five families? She who had been their slave for years was sorely missed. The lazy, useless womenkind had now to cook and bake, draw water and feed cows, and grumbled loudly and quarrelled savagely among themselves—yea, even to blows—though the task of one was now portioned among so many. The patient, graceful figure, toiling to and from the well, or laden with wood or fodder, was no longer to be met, and was missed by more than her own household.

"She was the fairest girl in all the district," said Gopal, the bunnia's son. "There was no joy in her life, she seemed glad to die. Truly her execution was a grand tamasha, and brought many strangers from afar."

This was her epitaph.

Jasoda's name is still green in the memory of the villagers of Sharsheo; not that they acknowledge any special claim on her part to beauty, virtue, or martyrdom, but simply because it is not easy to forget that Jasoda, the daughter of Akin-alloo, and the widow of Sapona, was hanged.

An Appeal to the Gods.

"We be the gods of the East,
Older than all;
Masters of mourning and feast,
How shall we fall?"

Within forty miles of where the Himalayas rise from the plains, and the sunrise unveils the blushing snows—and precisely half a koss from the Kanāt river—lies the hamlet of Haru, surrounded by a tangle of castor-oil plants, mango trees, and tamarinds, and standing in the midst of a fertile tract of cane, corn, and poppy. The scarlet-and-white poppies, the stiff, green cane, the waving yellow wheat, also the village (which boasted nine hundred souls at the last census), were the joint property of two wealthy zemindars. The northern part of Haru—including the crops sown for the opium department—was the inheritance of Durga Pershad, a tall, dark, gaunt man, with an unpleasant and sinister expression. The wheat, cane, and southern end of the town belonged to Golab Rai Sing, who bore but a scant resemblance to his name—"the King of Roses;" he was, in fact, a stout, smiling, pock-marked person, with a glib tongue, and a close fist. These two zemindars hated one another as thoroughly as men in their position were not only bound, but born to do. They had not merely been bequeathed adjoining lands, and a whole village between them, but a venerable blood feud, which had been conscientiously handed down from generation to generation.

In good old days—days within living memory—there had been desperate outbreaks, dacoities, and murders, attended with the usual sequel: hanging or imprisonment beyond the seas. Now, in more civilized times (although the vital question of the well by the temple was yet in abeyance, passed on from collector to collector), the rival factions were content with pounding each other's cattle, burning each other's fodder, and blackening each other's characters. Both had a large following of tenants, relations, parasites; and he who brought tidings that evil had befallen the enemy was a truly welcome guest! When the great men met, they simply scowled and passed on their way, and their women-folk laid every sin to the charge of their neighbours that it is possible for the depraved imagination of a practised native slanderer to conceive.

Golab Rai Sing was the richer of the two zemindars, though Durga Pershad owned a larger extent of ground; but it was whispered that he had lost much money in a law-suit, and that Muttra Dass (the soucar) held a mortgage on his best crops; nevertheless, he carried his head high, and his wife had real silver tyres to the wheels of her ekka!

It was the first moon in the new year, and the collector's camp was pitched under the mango tope, between the village and the river; he had but recently returned from two years' furlough, and from the whirl of politics and the turmoil of life at high pressure; also, he was new to the district.

As he stood meditating on the river bank at dawn, and saw the snows rise on the horizon with the sun, watched the strings of cattle soberly threading their way to pasture, heard the doves cooing in the woods, and the rippling of the river through the water plants, he said to himself, "Here at least is rest and peace." Casting his eyes toward the red-roofed houses, half concealed among bananas and cachar trees,—with their exquisite purple flowers—

"I am not sure that these people have not six to four the best of it," he remarked aloud (no one but his dog received this startling confidence), as he gazed enviously at a group of lean brown Brahmins who were dipping piously in the Kanāt, and pouring water from their brass lotahs; he thought of his own tailor's and other bills, his wife's insane extravagance, her flirtations, his hard work, his years of enforced exile.

"Yes," he continued, "*we* know nothing about it. We wear ourselves out running after phantoms. Here is contentment, assurance of future happiness, and present peace."

But then, you see, he was a new man—a visionary—and was totally ignorant of the internal condition of this picturesque and primitive hamlet.

The same day, as in duty bound, the two zemindars, each mounted on a pony, and followed by a crowd of retainers, waited upon the collector sahib, apparently on the most amicable terms. Just once a year they were compelled to masquerade as friends, though when they had the collector's ear in private audience, their mutual complaints were both numerous and bitter. They bore, as offerings, fruit and wreaths of evil-smelling marigolds (that noxious flower so amazingly dear to the native of India); also Golab Rai Sing carried with him one thing which his rival lacked, and that was his son and only child, Soonder—*i.e.* "the beautiful"—a lively boy of five years, who was gaily attired in a rose-coloured satin coat, and wore a purple velvet cap and gold bangles. He was a sharp and unquestionably spoiled urchin. He sat with his father and friends, or with his mother and her associates, and listening open-eared, like the proverbial little pitcher, heard many things that were not good for his morals—heard perpetual ridicule and abuse of the enemy of his house; therefore, when he encountered Durga Pershad in fields or byways, he made hideous grimaces at him, squinted significantly, and called him "dog," "pig," "robber"—behaviour that naturally endeared him to Pershad, who yearned with irrepressible craving to find him alone! Subsequently the heir of Golab Rai Sing would return to his fond parents, boast of his performance, and receive as reward and encouragement lumps of sticky cocoanut and deliciously long, wormy native sweets.

On the supreme occasion of the yearly reception, the child Soonder was as prettily behaved and hypocritical as his elders. The collector's lady noticed him—and that publicly. She knew better than to say he was a handsome boy (for, if she had no fear of the evil eye, it was otherwise with her audience), but she gave him a picture paper, and a battledore and shuttlecock, and his father swelled, beamed, and literally shone with pride—for was not the presentation made in the face of childless Durga Pershad, and all the elders of the people? And greater glory was yet in store for this fortunate zemindar. The collector, having looked over various papers, and heard witnesses (many false), actually deigned to visit the well in person, and concluded what he considered a shamefully procrastinated case, and finally made over the Kooah well, and all its rights, to Golab Rai Sing and his heirs for ever!

That night Golab made a great feast to all his followers, and bitter were the thoughts of his defeated rival, as he lay sleepless on his string charpoy, listening to the devilish exultation implied by the ceaseless tom-toms.

As days went on, his thoughts became still more poignant; it seemed to him that his friends were showing defection. Golab Rai had fine crops, on which there was no lien; he had a son to light the torch of his funeral pyre; he had the well. Of a truth, he had *too* much! And he, Pershad, had been flung in the dust, like a broken gurrah. Thus he reflected as he sat brooding on the river-bank at sundown. The cattle were strolling home through the marshes, the cranes were wheeling overhead, close by a fierce, lean, black pariah gnawed some mysterious and ghastly meal among the rushes, and on a sandbank lay three huge alligators—motionless as logs of wood—crafty as foxes, voracious as South Sea sharks. Durga Pershad glanced indifferently at the cattle, at the cranes, but as his eyes fell on the alligators they kindled, they blazed with a truly sinister flash—the alligators had offered him an idea!

* * * * *

It was the feast of lights or lanterns, the festival of Lucksmi, wife of Vishnu, and the goddess of festival. She, however, brought naught but sore misfortune to the house of Golab Rai, for since sundown the child was missing—was gone, without leaving a trace. Amongst the busy excitement of preparing the illuminations and decorations, he had vanished. His mother supposed he was with his father, and his father believed him to be with his mother. Every house, byre, and nook—

yea, even the well, was searched in vain. Durga Pershad was humbly appealed to, as he sat on his chabootra stolidly smoking his huka.

"Why question me?" he replied. "How should I know aught of the brat? What child's talk is this?"

A whole day—twenty-four long hours—elapsed, and suspicion pointed a steady finger at Durga Pershad. Of late it was noticed that he and the child had been friends—that he had given Soonder sweets—yea, and a toy. One man averred that he saw a pair resembling them going towards the river about sundown. The child was jumping for joy, and had a green air-balloon in his hand.

This, Durga Pershad swore, was a black lie; he had never left the village; his kinsman could speak.

"For how much?" scoffed the other side. "What fool will credit a man's relations?"

Four days passed, and Golab Rai had aged by twenty years. His round, fat face was drawn and shrivelled; he was bent like an aged man, and tottered as he walked.

As for his wife, she had almost lost her senses, though both she and her husband clung wildly to hope, and he had lavished money unsparingly in rewards and horse-flesh. As a last resource, the miserable mother of Soonder came and cast her dishevelled person at the feet of Durga Pershad—Durga Pershad, whom all her life she had mocked, reviled, and figuratively spat upon.

"Take all I possess!" she cried—"my jewels, my eyes, my very life; but tell me what thou hast done with him? Doth he yet live? My life, all thou wilt, for his!"

As she spoke, a little cap was brought—a velvet cap, soaking with water. It had been found by a fisherman three miles down the river.

This was sufficient answer to the question, "Doth he yet live?" The child was no more, his cap bore witness; and Gindia, his mother, swooned as one that was dead.

Yes, Soonder had been thrown to the alligators, without doubt; cast into their jaws, like a kid or a dog. In their mind's eye, the villagers beheld the hideous scene, they heard the shriek, saw the splash, and the ensuing scuffle. What death should Durga Pershad die?

The whole place was in an uproar; excitement was at fever heat. The police were sent for to Hassanpore, the nearest large station, and the suspected zemindar was marched away, and lodged in the Jail Khana; even his own people were dumb.

Durga Pershad stoutly avowed his innocence by every oath under a Hindoo heaven. He engaged, at enormous expense, an English pleader from Lucknow. He paid much money elsewhere. There was no case. If one man swore he met him with the child at sundown on the feast of lights, there were five unshaken witnesses who had seen him at the same hour in the village.

Therefore Durga Pershad was acquitted; and, moreover, in the words of the Sudder judge, "without a stain on his character!"

Nevertheless, matters were not made equally agreeable for him at home. His own partisans—save his tenants—held aloof with expressive significance, and those who were wont to assemble on his chabootra of an evening to smoke, argue, and bukh, were reduced by more than half.

But he held his head as high as ever, whilst that of his enemy lay low, even to the dust. Of what avail now to Golab Rai were his crops, his rents, his great jars of "ghoor" (coarse sugar), even his well, when he had no longer a child—a son and heir?

The immediate effects of the tragedy gradually faded away; it had ceased to be the sole daily topic, and it was again winter-time. One chill, starlight evening, as Durga Pershad was riding home alone among the cane-fields, he was suddenly set upon by a number of men, who had lain in ambush in the crops. A cloth was thrown over his head, he was dragged off his pony, and hustled into a doolie, which set off immediately, and at great speed. There were many riding and running beside it—the terrified prisoner heard the sound of steps and hoofs and muttered voices. It seemed to him that he travelled for days; but, in truth, he had only journeyed twenty hours, when he was suddenly set down, the sliding door was pushed back, and he was hauled forth. He found himself standing in a temple (an unknown temple), and by the light of blazing torches he recognized at least one hundred familiar faces, including those of Golab Rai and the priest of the village of Haru. He was so cramped and dazed that at first he could only stagger and blink; but as his hands were untied, he found his voice.

"What foul deed is this?" he demanded hoarsely. "Where am I?"

"Thou art within the most holy temple of Gola-Gokeranath," answered the priest, impressively. "We have appealed to man for justice—and in vain. Therefore, we now approach the gods! Is it not so, my brothers?"

The reply was a prolonged murmur of hoarse assent from the quiet, fierce-eyed crowd.

"Behold the image of Mahadeo, the destroyer!" continued the priest, pointing to a conical stone in the middle of the temple, on which the holy Ganges water dripped without ceasing. "Here is the mark of Hanuman's thumb, where he rested on his way to Ceylon to war against the great giant Ravan."

A venerable Mahant, or high-priest of the Gosains, now advanced, and said, in a voice tremulous with age—

"Lay thy hand upon this spot, O Durga Pershad, and swear as I shall speak."

Durga Pershad held back instinctively, but the pressure of fifty arms constrained him, and he yielded.

"If I have had part or lot in the death of Soonder, the son of Golab Rai Sing——"

There was an expressive pause for a full moment, and no sound was audible save the slow, monotonous dripping of the sacred stream.

Durga Pershad shuddered, but repeated the sentence somewhat unsteadily.

"—I call upon Mahadeo, the most holy, the destroyer, to smite me with the black leprosy in the sight of all men, and that within three moons. May I die in torture, and by piecemeal. May I be abhorrent alike to men and gods, and after death, may I hang by my feet for one thousand years above a fire of chaff."

Durga Pershad echoed this hideous sentence with recovered composure. Truly, it was a vast relief to find that his end was not yet—his life in no present danger.

Here was a weird and ghostly scene! The dark, damp temple, at dead of night, the crowd of stern, accusing countenances, lit up by flashes of torchlight, the austere high-priest in his robe of office, and the haggard culprit, the central figure, glaring defiance, with his uplifted hand upon the cold wet stone! There seemed to the wretched accused some accursed power in this holy image; the stone clung tenaciously to his trembling flesh, and he was sensible of an awful, death-like chill that penetrated to the very marrow of his bones.

* * * * *

In a few minutes the lights were extinguished, the wolfish-faced crowd had melted away, and Durga Pershad found himself alone. He stumbled out of the shrine, and by the cold, keen starlight descried the edge of a large tank, which was surrounded by temples. He had never visited the place of his own free will, but he recognized it from description as undoubtedly the most holy Gola, where two hundred thousand pilgrims flocked to worship once a year.

At daybreak he made his way to the bazaar, and there sold a silver chain,—for he had no money. It might be imagination, but he believed that people looked upon him with suspicious eyes. Three days later, he was at home once more. He told no one that he had been kidnapped—no, not even his mother or his wife.

By the end of a month, Durga Pershad had become an altered man. He looked wofully lean and haggard, he scarcely ate, slept, or smoked, and appeared dreadfully depressed. He now cared nought for taxes, rents, or crops, and complained of a strange numbness in his limbs. Much to the surprise of his household, he undertook a pilgrimage to Hurdwar, the source of the Ganges (some one had suggested most holy Gola—some one ignorant of Durga's enforced expedition). He had barely returned from Hurdwar when, as if possessed by a fever of piety, he set forth for Badrinath, in the Himalayas. After that long and arduous journey, he passed rapidly down to Benares. From thence, concluding an absence of four months, he returned finally to Haru, and shut himself up within his own courtyard and in his own house, refusing to see even his nearest of kin. And now it began to be whispered about from ear to ear that Durga Pershad, the son of Govindoo Pershad, was smitten with the kôrh—or black leprosy.

Yes, the grasp of that terrible disease was upon him. His features altered, thickened, and took the fatal and unmistakable leonine look. In a surprisingly short time he had lost the fingers of both hands. To show himself abroad would simply be to proclaim his guilt, and the judgment of Mahadeo—whose wrath he had invoked. For weeks and weeks he successfully evaded his enemies, fortified within his own house, and protected by his wife and mother, whose shrill tongues garrisoned it effectually.

When it became known that the hours of Durga Pershad were numbered, a body of the elders, led by the village priest, came and sternly demanded an entrance. They would take *no* denial. After frantic clamour and frenzied resistance, they gained admittance—admittance to the very presence of the leper, who lay in a darkened room, huddled up on a string bed.

"Behold," cried the priest in a sonorous voice, "the finger of Mahadeo, and the punishment of the slayer of a child! Speak, ere your tongue rot away, and declare unto us what befell the boy at thy hands, O Durga Pershad, leper!"

"Begone!" screamed his wife. "Depart, devil, born with the evil eye, come to mock at the afflicted of the gods!"

"When he hath spoken, we will go our ways," answered a solemn voice; "but otherwise, we remain until the end."

Durga Pershad raised himself laboriously on his charpoy; his head was muffled up in a brown blanket, he was nearly blind, and cried aloud, in a shrill, piercing falsetto—

"Yea, here is the answer—the god's answer"—and he thrust out a leprous arm—"I did it."

"How? Hasten to speak, O vile one!"

"I long desired his life," he panted. "He came with me to the river-bank of his own accord, for I had promised him a rare spectacle. My heart was hot within me—yea, as a red-hot horse-shoe. Even as he clamoured for my promise, I flung him to the alligators. It was over in a minute—but—I hear his scream now!"

Then Durga Pershad covered his face, and lo! as he turned to the wall, he died.

Two Little Travellers.

CHAPTER I.

Gram had fallen to nine seers for the rupee, which affected the sahibs who kept horses and polo ponies; and rice was down to eight measures—this affected the villagers and ryots. The rains due at Christmas had failed. There was talk of a great scarcity and a sore famine in the land, especially among the sleek, crafty bunnias, who bought up every ounce of grain in the district when it was cheap, and at the first whisper of failing crops—often a rumour started by themselves—locked it up relentlessly, in hopes of starvation prices, refusing to sell save at exorbitant rates.

What is a road coolie to do under these conditions?—a man whose daily wage never exceeds one anna and a half, no matter how markets may fluctuate. Three rupees' worth of grain will keep him alive for twenty days; but how is he to exist for the remainder of the month? How is he to feed his children, to pay his tiny rental, and the village tax?

This was a problem that Chūnnee pondered over, as he sat on a heap of stones at the side of the road, with his empty basket at his feet, and a look of despair upon his handsome, and usually good-humoured, countenance.

Alas! Chūnnee had been born under an evil star. Scorpio was his constellation, and all the luck had ebbed from him, as surely as it had flowed towards his half-brother Zālim Sing.

Now, Zālim Sing was prosperous and well-to-do, the proprietor of a good mud house, a patch of castor oil, and two biggahs of land, planted in rape and linseed; he also owned a huge milch buffalo, a pair of plough bullocks, and the only ekka within three koss. Yes, an ekka that came to him with his wife, all lavishly decorated with brass knobs and ornamental work, an ekka that had yellow curtains, and was drawn by a bay tat (a bazaar pony), with six rows of blue beads round her ewe neck. Zālim Sing was prouder of his turn-out than any parvenu's wife with her first equipage; and perhaps it was on the strength of this, more than his store of linseed and his plot of land, that the village elders hearkened to him with respect. He was a lean, shrewd-looking man, with a cast in his eye and a halt in his gait. Nevertheless, he had prospered, and the world had gone well with him, whereas it had gone ill with his half-brother.

But Chūnnee was not wise in his generation; he had bartered away his share of the ancestral home for two cows, a grindstone, and some brass cooking-pots. The cows had died the rains before last, the cooking-pots were pawned to the local soucar; his crop of one mango tree had failed, he had no capital except his sturdy frame, two horny hands, and his coolie basket.

In his hovel there were his children—Girunda, a boy aged ten, and Gyannia, a girl of four. There was also a mat, an old charpoy, a reaping-hook, a couple of earthen pots, and a white cat. This was all that Chūnnee possessed in the wide world. It might have sufficed, had he had wisdom like his brother; but, alas! he had no brains. There he sat, on the kunker heap, that glaring February afternoon. The land was still covered with cane crops; the barley was green, and in the ear; dry leaves were whirling along the road; the banka tree was dropping red flowers from its grey, leafless branches; the mango tree was in blossom. Yes, the hot weather, the time of parching and scarcity, would be on them soon. Suddenly he heard a rattling, and felt a cloud of warm yellow dust. It was his brother's ekka. Zālim Sing and a friend tore past at a gallop, and scarcely noticed the coolie on the side of the road, beyond a hoarse laugh of derision. Why had fortune been kind to one brother and cruel to another? Why had his cows died?—his wife been bitten by a "karite" as she cut vetches, and expired at sundown in agonies? Ah, Junia was a loss—nigh as great as the cows. She cooked, and minded the children; she earned one anna a day for reaping; she was fortunate to die young; she had never lived to know hunger. Why had some people stores and treasures, to whom they were of no use, whilst others lacked a morsel to keep them from perishing?

Chūnnee sat for half an hour with his arms loosely folded on his breast, and pondered this question in his heart. Presently he arose, and picked up his basket, and took the path towards his village, where its brown mud walls and straw roofs stood out in strong relief against a noble tope of mango trees; but these mangoes were the property of the sirkar (government). Many an envious eye had been cast on them and their fine yearly harvests. Despite bazaar rumours about scarcity, it was surely what is called a bunnia's famine; for this hungry, handsome Rajpoot, with the form and sinews of some Greek god, made his way homewards between marvellous crops at either side of the well-beaten path. The self-same rich land was yielding gram, rape, linseed; whilst barley towered high above all. Where else will the earth yield four harvests with little manure or care? But not an inch of this fertile soil called Chūnnee master! And what to him was all this fertility? As he strode along, a fierce temptation kept pace with his steps, and whispered eagerly in his ear—

"There is old Turroo, thy great-uncle; he is nigh ninety years of age, and rich;

his head was grey in the mutiny year. True, he favours Zālim Sing. They say he hath even advanced him money for seeds, because he is prosperous; and he will not look at thee, because thou art poor, much less suffer thee to cross his threshold. They declare he hath a treasure buried—some that he came upon in the mutiny year. What avails it to him? He hath his huka and his opium, his warm bedding, and brass cooking-pots. He only enjoys money when he looks at it—and thy children are starving. They say that thousands of rupees are hidden under his floor, and one hundred rupees would make thee a rich man. Thou mightest till that plot of ground near the big baal tree, and buy two plough bullocks for twenty-five rupees. Krisna would then lend thee his plough. Set grain—not linseed, having no mill—grain at even twelve seers next year, and thou wilt be a wealthy man; yea, and better than Zālim Sing, who will no longer scoff at thee or cover thee with dust. Thou wilt have no need to go out as coolie. Thou wilt have plenty of flour, and dál, and fresh tobacco in thy huka. It is easy—as easy as breathing. But to rob—to rob an old man?" inquired conscience. "True; but thine own kinsman, who cannot carry his money to the burning ghâut, it ought to be thine some day. Thou art his heir, though he hates thee—men often hate their next-of-kin. His hoarding—it is of no use to him—it will save thee and thine from death."

"But how—how can I take it?" inquired Chūnnee of the tempter.

"Behold, the nights are dark, the moon doth not rise till morn; thou hast thy krooplie still; dig through the mud wall. They say the box is buried near the hearth; open it, and carry away what thou wilt in thy cloth. The old man sleeps as though a corpse—he drinks opium. He has no one in the house, no dog. It is so easy; truly, it is a marvel he hath not been robbed before! Take it; be bold. Truly, it is half thine. Thou canst keep a pony, too, and buy silver bangles for Gyannia."

"But how can I account for this sudden wealth? All the world knows that I am but a beggar."

"Carry it forth and hide it, bury it in a hole far away; for doubtless there will be a great search. Some weeks later, take a few rupees, and go by rail to Lucknow; and come back, and say thy wife's grandmother hath died, and left thee one hundred rupees. The gold and jewels thou wilt take in a roll of bedding to Lucknow, and sell. It will all be easy; have no fear."

As these ideas were working in his brain, and he was the sport of two conflicting feelings, Chūnnee was rapidly approaching his little hovel, which lay on the outskirts of the village of Paroor. It was a small hamlet of mud houses, huddled together most irregularly. There was no main street, nor even an attempt at one; no chief entrance—merely half a dozen footpaths running into the village from various directions. There would be a high mud wall and doorway leading into an enclosure, containing twenty small huts, and as many families, all connected; here were also ponies, calves, fowl, the property of the clan, and perchance a bullock-cart or a sugar-press. These enclosures were set down indiscriminately, and joined together; the only village street, an irregular path, that threaded its way between them. There were "sets" even here, as in higher circles; inmates of one mud courtyard, who owned a sugar-press, looked down on the inmates of those who had none.

Most people looked down on Chūnnee, the coolie—even the women, although he was a handsome, well-made fellow. What are looks, when a man has not a pice, and owns nought save two crying children? Chūnnee made his way past a crowd collected round a khooloo, or sugar-mill—a rude, wooden affair, turned by two bullocks, fed with bits of raw cane, which it squeezes into a receptacle in the ground, and subsequently empties into another vat indoors, where the sugar is boiled, and finally poured off into huge jars (similar to those which contained the forty thieves), and sent to middlemen, who thereby reap much profit. Paroor was in the midst of a sugar country, and boasted half a dozen of these rude sugar-mills.

Chūnnee passed through the scattered strips of cane, basket in hand—there were no greetings for him—and, turning a corner, dived between two mud walls into a small hut that stood by itself. A slim, nearly naked lad ran out to meet him, with a look of expectation on his intelligent face, but, alas! his father was empty-handed. On the mat lay a little girl with curly hair and a fair but puny face. She was fast asleep, holding in her arms a miserably thin bazaar kitten—or it might be a full-grown cat stunted in size.

"She was hungry; I fetched her some banka fruit from cows—now she is asleep," explained the boy. "There is a little barley—the last—I made it," and he pointed to a cake, a very small one, baking on some embers.

"Father, what shall we do to-morrow?" he asked, as his father devoured the only food he had seen that day.

"There is still the reaping-hook."

"Gunesh offers two annas for it."

"And it cost a rupee and a half."

"I went to-day to old Turroo, to ask him for a few cowries, or a bit of a chupatti for Gyannia—she was crying with hunger, and calling for food."

"And what did he give thee?"

"He smote me a blow on the back with his staff"—pointing to a weal on his shoulder. "He said I was a devil's spawn, good for nothing; like thee—a beggar."

"I would not be as I am, but I have never had a chance—never one chance." And, ravenous as he was, Chūnnee the famished yielded half his cake in answer to his son's wistful and expectant eyes.

When darkness had fallen on the village, the inhabitants went to bed like the birds—it saved oil—though there were a few budmashes who sat up all night and gambled; each visiting the other's house in turn, and providing light and drink. Yes, drink—drink, from the fatal mowra tree. The fever of gambling seemed to be all over the land. Some gambled away their money, clothes, tools, cattle, but this gang kept their proceedings secret—yea, even from their nearest neighbours. Chūnnee had never gambled.

As, by degrees, the children were called in, and the houses shut, the village grew dark and quiet. About twelve o'clock, Chūnnee rose, and felt for his krooplie (a mattock with a short handle); then he opened the door and looked forth; there was not a sound to be heard, save the breathing of the children and the distant howling of a pack of jackals. There were the clear cold stars in the sky, showing above the opposite wall. Should he do it? Oh, if Heaven would but send him a sign! It seemed to him that his devout wish was instantly fulfilled, for at that moment Gyannia turned in her sleep, moaning her frequent and pitiful cry when awake, "I am hungry."

CHAPTER II.

Chūnnee had now received his answer; he stole forth, and crept like a shadow from wall to wall, down a series of narrow paths, till he came to a house standing alone in an open space—a notable abode, for a tree grew through the roof. There was no gate to the outer yard, no dog. The door was closed—needless to try it; he must work his way through the mud wall at the back, and crawl in. The baking of many seasons' suns had effectually hardened this impediment, and he strove for an hour, listening for sounds with intense trepidation, whilst the sweat poured down his face. At last he had scraped a sufficiently large aperture—he was slender to leanness. He crept through, but his usual bad luck pursued him; his head came violently against a brass chattie that fell with a clang enough to waken the dead. It effectually aroused the old man, who awoke and struck a match, and showed Chūnnee that he had come too late!

The light displayed a deep hole in the floor, an empty hole. The door was ajar; the treasure was already stolen; and Chūnnee stood there, krooplie in hand, with the cavity in the wall to speak for him—the convicted thief!

Old Turroo's piercing shrieks of "murder" and "dacoity" assembled a dozen people in less than three minutes. Yea, truly, he had been robbed! A box lay outside empty, and Chūnnee the coolie, the ne'er-do-well, had come to this!

He was caught like a rat in a trap! There was the opening in the wall, the muddy krooplie in his grasp; he stood plainly convicted. The criminal hung his head—of what avail to speak, and aver his innocence?—he was not innocent! Others had got the booty, he would suffer for them. As he had been toiling and labouring they had been within, and had carried off what he too had come to seek.

Perhaps he was served rightly; but he never got a chance—no, not even to rob.

Meanwhile old Turroo literally rent his clothes, and tore his scanty white beard, and howled, cursed, and gesticulated like a madman. Zālim Sing stood foremost amongst sympathizers (for the venerable relative still possessed a house, cattle, and lands), and said "that truly it did not surprise him to find that the thief was his blood-brother."

Nevertheless, it did astonish most of the assembly, for Chūnnee, if miserably poor, had ever been known to be scrupulously honest. They were amazed, moreover, that he should *begin* on such a large scale! Chūnnee offered no resistance; he was led away, and shut up in a cowhouse, whilst Zālim Sing's brother-in-law, full of zeal, ran all the way to Bugwa to fetch the police.

The police arrived at daybreak—two men and an inspector, in their blue tunics and red turbans—all looking excessively wise; but their searching and cross-examining, discovered nothing beyond the empty box. How had Chūnnee spirited away the treasures? Who was his accomplice?

"Let him be beaten till he speaks," implored the venerable creature who had been ravished of his treasure. "Let the soles of his feet be roasted until he opens his mouth. Where hath he hidden them?"—and he shouted to the whole assembled village—"the two bags of rupees, the golden bangles, the anklets, the strings of pearls—forty pair without blemish? If he will only give me the pearls!"—and the old man lifted up his voice and wept.

A dirty, half-naked old man, how strange it seemed, to behold him weeping for his pearls! Now, had it been a young and lovely woman, the grief would have seemed natural. And who would have believed that old Turroo had such treasures? Ay, he was a sly fox.

"Give me my pearls, yea, and my gold mohurs. Thou mayst keep the rest, and go free," he declared magnanimously.

But Chūnnee could not give what he had not got, and therefore held his peace. His children screamed when they saw their father's arms pinioned with ropes, the iron things on his hands, and heard he was going away to the Jail Khana—screamed from fear and hunger.

Meanwhile old Turroo howled and raved like one possessed, and, pointing to his grand-nephew, besought the police to put him to torture by fire, then and there. In former days strange things were done under the mantle of the law; but in these enlightened times no policeman dare venture, even for a large bribe, to practise the question by torture.

So Chūnnee was led away captive, followed as far as the high-road by fully half the village; and for more than a mile along that dusty track, two little weeping creatures pattered behind him. At length the girl could go no further, and fell exhausted. Her father halted between his guard, and said—

"Girunda, take care of thy sister. Go to thy uncle; he will feed thee till I come back. Go now, ere nightfall."

And if he doth not receive them, what is to become of them? was a thought that harassed him all the weary march. At a turn of the road he turned and looked back, and saw the two small forlorn figures standing in the straight, white highway, watching him to the last.

Chūnnee was brought up before the magistrate that day. He had been taken red-handed, and had not denied his guilt. He was silent with respect to the treasure. It had been a most daring dacoity, but, as it was his first offence, he would be only sentenced to two years' imprisonment in Shahjhanpur jail.

"And his two children?" he ventured to ask. "Who would care for them? How were they to live?" (There are no poor-houses in India.)

"Oh, the neighbours, or your relations," said the Sudder judge, knowing how immensely generous, good, and charitable the very poorest are to one another. "You have a brother, of course—he will take them."

Chūnnee was by no means so sanguine on this point.

He was sent on foot to jail—a distance of sixty miles—and there put in leg-irons, and a convict sacking-coat, with a square cap to cover his shaven head. He was set to work to pick oakum. He worked steadily, though with a face and air of dogged despair. But what was the good of giving trouble? What was the good of anything? The jail fare was not jail fare to him—it was better than he had at home; and now that he had sufficient to eat, he grew strong. But how were his children faring? Were they starving? Other convicts—robbers, gamblers, dacoits—thought Chūnnee proud and sullen, he was so silent; or surely he was in for some great crime?

Luckily for him, the jail daroga liked him, and promoted him to basket-making, and thence to the vegetable garden. His percentage on his earnings he did not take out in money, or even in the Sunday smoke. No; all went to the remission of his sentence. Truly, life was not so bad, save for the hangings—every convict was forced to attend—and these executions were not infrequent, for Shahjhanpur was in the centre of a district notorious for murders. It was a veritable case of "Satan finds some mischief still for idle hands to do."

When all the grain of this most fertile tract is harvested, and the sugar-cane brakes have been cut and carried away on bullock-carts, when the linseed is pressed, and the sugar sold, and the wheat threshed and ground, it is the hot weather; no sowing or ploughing can be done. People must wait for the first burst of the rains, to soften the stone-like ground. And, oh, how sweet to the nostrils is the smell of earth after the first wild downpour!

Meanwhile, they have money in their hands—the fruit of their labour. They have long, hot, idle days, and no occupation, so they rake up old land-feuds, old blood-feuds, old jealousies, and the result is but too frequently a man's body found in a nullah, killed by a sickle or a lathi (heavy stick), or a woman's corpse drawn out of some abandoned well.

The jail gardens supplied all the vegetables to the station, and the mem sahibs, when the vegetable "doli" came late, knew well the reason—there had been a hanging.

Chūnnee attended the first execution with apparently more trepidation than the criminal himself, who walked to his fate with a jaunty air, and on being asked if he had arranged all his affairs said—

"By your favour, yea;" and then, on second thoughts, added, with amazing vivacity, "There is one small brass lotah which I forgot. I desire that it be given to my sister-in-law." And so, singing a song to Nirvana, he ascended the gallows and calmly met his fate.

Another young man's demeanour was outrivalled by that of his own father and the kinsfolk who had come to take leave of him.

The execution was at half-past six, and the official in charge—a tender-hearted gentleman—stood waiting till the farewells were over, watch in hand. Time was up, but he would give this vigorous young Brahmin yet a few more minutes of life. He was engaged in eager conversation with his relatives, and it was commonly reported and suspected that he had actually confessed to the crime, and sacrificed himself in order to save a near kinsman. The official glanced at his watch once more, and was astounded to catch the eye of the culprit's father, and hear him say, in a most matter-of-fact tone—

"Yea, truly, my son, time is up. Thou hadst better go at once, for, remember, we have fifteen koss to carry thee to the Ganges to burn—and we shall not get home till dark, and the moon is old!"

The son, without a word, salaamed to this more than Roman parent, and then turned to meet his fate without an instant's hesitation. Chūnnee had beheld many heroes of this type, but he had also seen others who had not had it in them to encounter death with similar fortitude. He had noted the wandering, terrified eye, the ashen lips drawn back from the chattering teeth, the twitching knee-caps, as the man was led forth to die like a dog; he had seen it, and the sight had made his heart melt like wax within him, and his limbs shake as if he had been stricken with palsy. It was his one horror, to be warned to attend an execution.

And then there was the ever-haunting fear about his two desolate, helpless children—were they well or ill, alive or dead? He was seventy-six miles from his own pergunnah—no one ever visited him with tidings from home, no one came to see him, and brought him bazaar news, and sweets, a tin pot to drink from, or even a bit of a wheaten chupatti. No, he had no friends, either within the jail, or beyond its walls.

CHAPTER III.

Meanwhile the desolate little couple had toiled painfully back to Paroor, and halted outside their uncle's enclosure. They dared not venture in, and they crouched timidly without the battered wooden doorway, whilst Zālim Sing laid down the law, expounded his own virtues, and denounced Chūnnee to more than half the village. He had always been secretly jealous of his good-looking brother, who, moreover, was the father of a son, whilst his wife had borne him, instead of the much-desired heir, no fewer than seven daughters, of whom four survived; and Zālim's enemies said among themselves that his sins must be many, or he would never have been punished with seven girls! He talked freely, knowing there was no one to defend the absent, and the starving pair heard that their father was a liar, a dacoit, a budmash, a thief, and the most ungrateful kinsman to a noble-hearted brother that ever drew the breath of life—one cannot talk for ever; and as the listeners gradually dropped off, notice was naturally attracted by the two wretched little beggars in the lane—what was to become of them?—their home was empty, save for a reaping-hook, a charpoy, and a cat.

Zālim Sing pulled his beard, and scowled; his crooked eye rolled fiercely, till a woman in the crowd exclaimed in a loud clear voice—

"Since thou sayest thou art a benevolent man, and the most generous of kinsmen, why dost thou stare at the starving ones, instead of taking them in?"

Their dusty feet and hunger-stricken faces touched the crowd—as easily swayed as the branch of a tree to this side and that, by whatever wind may blow.

There was a hoarse murmur, which the crafty Zālim quickly interpreted; now was the time to pose as a noble benefactor—or never; and he drew the two children over the threshold of the door, and shut himself in with his detested encumbrances.

He gave them some coarse food and water, and showed them a sort of shed where they might sleep. "But thou mayst not enter my house," he said, "or play with my children; thy father is a wicked man, therefore ye are pariahs, but I and my children are good."

The next day he went to his brother's abode and sold the old charpoy, reaping-hook, and house for the sum of seven rupees; but he could neither sell nor kill the cat—she sat serenely aloft in a neem tree, far out of his reach. Presently she discovered her old owners, or they discovered her; they hid her secretly in their miserable shelter, and begged a little milk in the village. Alas! she was their only friend. Their cousins—four sallow, ugly children, two of whom had inherited their parent's violent squint, and all of whom were laden with anklets and bangles, and a vast sense of their own importance—condescended to come and patronize the two wicked beggars who lived in the old goat-shed in a corner of the enclosure. They experienced an intense and novel delight in patronizing, teasing, pinching, and threatening these little pariahs, who were better fun, and afforded more scope for amusement, than any of their usual games, and their sense of their own superiority swelled to enormous proportions. They visited the unfortunates at all hours; but the cat knew their voices, and hid hastily among the thatch. Bazaar cats are wonderfully active and cunning, they are also marvellous thieves, and the cat throve.

Presently Zālim Sing's wife discovered that Girunda was old enough to be of use. She set him to do the work of two servants, or one pony. He had to draw water and carry it home from the well, to grind corn, to cut fodder, whilst his little sister cried herself to sleep alone, for she dared not leave the cat, lest her ever-prying cousins should discover it and throw it down the well. Certainly its appearance was against it; it was lean and long and dirty-white, with a thin rat tail; and a sharp-pointed face—a pure village type—hungry, and careless of its appearance, a merciless mouser, but a faithful adherent.

Poor Girunda now toiled early and late, he received nought but blows, abuse, and the coarsest fare. Much of his utility was unknown to his uncle—who was frequently from home—but who scowled every time that his glance fell upon him.

Affairs were not going quite as smoothly as hitherto with Zālim Sing. The prices had risen in everything, save in his own particular commodity, linseed. There was the prospect of an unusually hot, scarce season, and his pony was sick. He vented all his ill humour on the two oppressed children "within his gates"—a most excellent, comprehensive, and Eastern expression—meaning within the mud or stone enclosure, where the master is supreme, where he can shut out all the world save his household, his oxen, and servants—shut it out by merely closing to the street an iron-knobbed wooden door. Within Zālim's gates his nephew became a slave; he was made to tend the furnace in the wall, at the other side of which boiled an enormous receptacle of linseed oil. This duty was murderous in the glaring, breathless month of April; it was worse than a fireman's work in June in the Red Sea—and the fireman is relieved at his post; no one ever relieved Girunda—the name signified "thick bread;" but of any bread his share was small—and then he fell sick. For two days he lay in his shed, burning with fever, his uncle beat him repeatedly with a thick stick for his laziness—beat him savagely too—but the boy made no moan, only his little sister screamed, and the screams attracted the neighbours.

"He is a lazy, idle, good-for-nothing pig!" explained the uncle to an eager inquirer; "he will not work aught save his teeth. And she is half-witted."

"True," said the listener; "and it is only a charitable man like thyself, O Zālim Sing, who would keep the beggar's brats, and with a dearth in the land, too; and wheat rising every week."

Then she went back to her spinning of coarse country cloth; Girunda lay and buried his head in his hands, and Gyannia sobbed in a corner; but his tormentor went into the house, to confer with his wife.

"If the boy would not work, neither should he eat. Was *he* himself to mind the furnace?" he demanded angrily.

"The boy is sickening," said the woman. "I have seen it coming—it is something bad—maybe the cholera, maybe the smallpox. It is surely some heavy sickness."

"And he may die?"

"Yea, having given it to us and ours. What shall we do?"

"Behold, to-night, when the village is quiet, I will take the two of them, and set them on the high-road. Thou canst bake some chupattis, and I will give them four annas, and tell them to begone, to return here no more, for if they do, of a surety I will kill them."

"They will believe thee!" said his wife with a laugh.

"Yea. Why should they not beg, as others do? And soon the boy can work, and earn an anna a day."

"Yea, he will soon be able to work," agreed this treacherous woman.

The children were surprised to be left in peace till sunset, and then to receive some fried beans and a chupatti—most sumptuous fare for them! But when it was dark, save for a dying moon, Zālim Sing entered their hut, staff in hand, and awoke them roughly.

"Arise quickly, and come with me; thou shalt no more remain under my roof. I have fed thee for three moons, now thou mayst go forth and feed thyselves. I will set thee on the road, and give thee food for two days and a little money; get thee to some town, and appeal to the charitable. Return here, and I will slay thee."

The children rose trembling; they had not much delay in dressing, but Gyannia smuggled the cat under her bit of blue cloth (once her mother's), and without one word the wretched pair meekly followed their uncle across the enclosure, past the oil-press, the sleeping bullocks, out of the postern, and through the silent village, then away to the high-road. Their kinsman walked along behind them in the powdery-white dust, stick in hand, for nearly two miles. It was nigh dawn; already the yellow light glimmered in the east; he must return; so he halted abruptly, and gave the boy some chupattis rolled in plantain leaves, and a four-anna piece (fivepence), and then said, "There lieth thy road out into the world; get thee gone, and never let me behold thy face again," and turning, he walked rapidly homewards.

The soft tap of his stick gradually died away, and then the children were quite alone. They sat down, and began to whisper. It was not a dream; their uncle had come to them in the middle of the night, and brought them along the high-road in the dark, and given them food, and told them to begone, and never let him see them again.

After their first feeling of astonishment had abated, they devoured a chupatti, sharing it with the cat; and then, as the dawn of light showed red along the horizon, they rose and went forward.

"If they had to walk, best make the journey now," thought the boy, who was wonderfully sensible for his years.

"Brother, whither are we going?" asked Gyannia presently.

"We have no one to go to but father," he replied. "We will go to him—to the Jail Khana."

But he did not tell her, nor would she have understood, that the jail in which their father lay imprisoned was seventy miles away. Hand-in-hand the two outcasts went slowly along the shadeless white roads; several villagers on the way to their work met them, and halted and stared at the party—a ragged little boy and girl, with a bazaar cat running after them.

CHAPTER IV.

That day Girunda and Gyannia walked five miles, resting in a nullah, under tufts of high grass, in the heat of the sun from nine till six—during which time the fierce hot winds roared over the land, and swept the roasted leaves up and down the roads, and shook the branches of the cork trees. How hot it was—every living thing seemed to have secured some shelter, save these forlorn children. The air was like a blast from a furnace, the very stones were scorching to the touch, and in the shallows, where a great river had rushed in the rains, there were now but a few shrunken pools in a stony bed; in these pools wallowed blue buffaloes (their hideous noses scarcely above water), enjoying a sort of tepid relief.

That night the travellers halted in a village; a gwali's (cowherd's) wife was surprised to see an exhausted-looking boy carrying on his back a little girl, the little girl in her turn carrying a cat. She invited them in, and gave them milk, and asked from whence they came.

"Paroor," replied Girunda.

"Paroor? Lo! it is six koss away. Do thy people know?" She eyed him with suspicion.

"Yea; our uncle hath turned us out to beg."

"And where art thou going?"

"To Shahjhanpur, where our father dwells."

"Shahjhanpur!" with a scream; "why, it is nigh thirty koss, and thou canst not walk there."

"There is no other means."

"Hast thou any money?"

Girunda untied a rag, and proudly displayed his precious four-anna bit. He had never possessed such a sum in his life.

"It may maintain thee for two or three days," said the woman dubiously.

"What work is thy father doing in Shahjhanpur?"

"Some one said he was making matting," rejoined the boy, simply. "He is in jail."

"In jail! Oh, ye fathers!"

"Yea; he went three months ago."

"And what hath he done?—murder—robbery?"

"He hath done naught. They just took him."

"But surely he must have robbed or plundered?"

"Nay; he was always very poor. He had nothing to leave us but a sickle and this cat; but old Turroo Sing had all his money stolen."

"I see. And now it is buried somewhere," she added significantly. "How long will thy father be in jail?"

"Two years."

"A great time! Well, thou art weary, and must need rest. Lie here on this mat, and to-morrow I will give thee food to take thee on for a day or two—money I have none—and God will do the rest."

The next morning the children fared well. That good Samaritan, the gwali's wife, secured them seats in a passing bullock-hackery, and thus they accomplished a considerable distance.

The following day they met no friends, and the heat was frightful—the air like a flame. Nevertheless, Girunda tottered doggedly forward, with his sister on his back, for five miles, with long, long rests; and at sunset they were nearing a large native town—at any rate, it seemed large to them. They were sent to the serai—a resting-place for native wayfarers. There was a great entrance gate leading into a wide enclosed space, with plenty of accommodation for camels, ekkas, and horses, and little niches, or rooms, all around, for the travellers. This was indeed a new life to Girunda—his sister was asleep. He went and watched the hairy Punjaubi dealers watering and feeding their ponies; the bearded camel-men giving fodder to their screaming, bubbling, discontented animals; the "purda nashins," women, hidden behind a kind of screen in a corner, from whence came much shrill laughing and chattering. Tired as he was, he was still more curious, and crept forward and tried to peep, but was rewarded with a stinging blow and a volume of abuse from a hideous old hag. "They were all ugly," so he assured a hawker, who laughed at his discomfiture.

This serai, with its crowds of travellers, and groups of animals, and imposing entrance, was truly a most novel and wonderful scene to this ignorant village lad.

A woman, woman-like, once more took pity on the party—the queer little group of a boy and a girl and a cat, with no one belonging to them, and not even possessing a bundle of clothes. In reply to their petition, "O mother, will you help us?" she gave them a ride on her jingling ekka for about eight miles. Girunda and Gyannia had never been in (to them) such a splendid equipage before, and were extremely happy as the wiry chesnut animal between the shafts, who tasted naught but bad grass or roadside nibblings, kept up a steady canter mile after mile. But, alas! the ekka's owner was going in a different direction from theirs, and at a certain bridge she set them down, and took leave of them, turning away into a "cutcha" track.

They were now in a different country, where the road ran quite straight between lines of neem trees, and was bounded with burnt-up, rusty grass. The landscape was desolate; there were no villages peeping out of the clumps of trees, no houses by the roadside: but these are always rare in India.

They halted at sundown, and crept under the arches of a bridge over a dry watercourse, and ate raw rice and drank water. It was plain that they must pass the night where they were, and as they were very tired, they were not long in falling asleep. Gyannia, infant-like, slept soundly till dawn, but not so her brother. At midnight he was awoke by a cold, damp nose being poked into his face; he started up trembling, and a few minutes later he heard his visitor's melancholy cry—it was only a prowling jackal. As he sat and stared into the grey light, his sharpened ears heard another sound that made his heart beat very fast—the "haunk—haunk" of a hyena. The cat, too, sat up and listened. If it came their way, he had no weapon; and stories of children devoured by hyenas were a common topic among the crones of Paroor village. He had several times seen a hyena skulking round, when he was driving home the cow—a hideous, high-shouldered, shuffling brute; but then his father had been near, and he was not afraid. Now, alas! his father was miles away, and he was almost sick with terror. The cry came nearer and nearer—oh, fearfully near—now it was directly overhead! What intense relief! the brute was on the high-road right above them; yes, and the "haunk—haunk" was dying gradually away in the distance; but Girunda slept no more that night. Supposing it should come back? The cat, too, appeared to have anxieties; she did not curl up, but sat bolt erect beside him. She was a queer animal, attached to people and not to a place, though the first day she had followed them in a devious and uncertain manner, uttering low mews of expostulation, and even sitting down in the middle of the road, and thus remonstrating from afar, till they were almost out of sight, but subsequently joining them like a whirlwind, with a long white tail. Lately she had been carried, and had had "lifts" in the bullock-cart and ekka; so the cat was much the freshest of the party, and seemed to have become reconciled to the journey, though she evidently did not approve of sleeping out at night in the neighbourhood of hyenas.

It was the end of June, just before the rains broke; the sky was like molten brass, the earth like stone. Who would travel in such a time?—who but two homeless unfortunates, who must press forward or else lie down and perish! Girunda staggered along, carrying his sister, at the rate of three koss a day. The four annas were long exhausted, and they now openly begged their bread! Some gave them a few handsful of rice,—which they ate raw—some a few cowries, which they spent at the little bunnia shops; they could barely keep body and soul together! Yes, they were like the mendicants that had come to their own door in the good times Girunda remembered, when his mother was alive—and the cow.

His mother—he could recollect her well. She had pretty white teeth, and she laughed often; but one day she came back from the fields between two women. She was weeping, and so were they, and they sent him across the river to play; and when he returned, a boy in the village ran shouting to meet him, and cried, "Thy mother is dead; a snake bit her."

Sometimes Girunda thought he would die too; he was so hot, and so tired, and his feet were so sore. If only he could reach his father first! But how long the miles had become! How he strained his eyes to catch sight of the next milestone! and what an enormous time it seemed before it came into view! The road never varied—never turned to the right hand or the left; sometimes, as he toiled on, his poor tired brain imagined that it had taken the form of a great grey serpent, and was coming towards him to swallow him up. They were now within five miles of Shahjhanpur city—would he ever reach it? There were fine trees lining the route; there were plenty of ekkas and ponies; there was a loud-puffing fire-devil going yonder over a bridge (he had heard of it), with a lot of black boxes behind it; and still he was three miles from Shahjhanpur—now two. Oh, he could never arrive there—never!

CHAPTER V.

About half-past six o'clock the next morning a gang of convicts were working on the road near the jail, carrying stones with much chain-clanking, all obtrusively industrious for the moment, as the keen black eye of the jail burkundaz was fixed upon them; but presently his gaze was attracted by a little group that approached him: a policeman escorting two ragged children.

"What are these?" he inquired.

"They were found last night near the police thana on the Futupore Road. The boy had fainted on the wayside, and I kept them till dawn, when I brought them in on a passing hackery. They come, they say, from Paroor, a village seventy miles off. The boy has walked all the way, carrying the girl on his back—so he says."

"Truly, but it is a fable! Of a surety, they are beggars from our own city."

"We can easily prove them. They have come hither to seek their father, who is in prison here; they aver that his name is Chūnnee Sing, of Paroor."

The convicts lagged to listen, and one whispered to another, "It is the tall man, who never smiles."

"Such a one is here for dacoity—two years' sentence."

"Where is he?" inquired the burkundaz of one of the gang.

"Working in the jail-garden gang, hazoor" (*i.e.* your highness).

An order was given to fetch him at once.

"They had a cat, too," continued the policeman; "I left it at the thana. What do these beggars with a cat?"

Meanwhile a large crowd had collected round the children—the curly-haired, pretty little girl, and the miserably emaciated boy, with his lacerated feet tied up in rags—a number of market coolies and officers' servants; and the convicts dawdled near—as closely as they dared.

In a very short time the warder returned, preceded by a tall convict. The children stared with wistful, questioning eyes; they did not recognize Chūnnee, at first glance, in the close-fitting cap drawn well over his ears, his loose dress, and chains; but after a pause of breathless amazement he cried, "Array khoda! Girunda and Gyannia, my children, how came you here?"

They rushed to him at the sound of that familiar voice, and broke into loud cries and sobs—sobs of joy and relief.

"I walked," panted the boy presently, "and carried her. Uncle thrust us forth one night; he said he would kill us if we ever went back, so we came to thee. We will abide with thee; we will never leave thee," sobbed the boy, clinging to his hands, whilst Chūnnee took the girl up in his arms and fondled her.

"We are so tired and hungry, father; may we not go to thy house and rest?" and Gyannia dropped her head on his shoulder.

The jail official was much perplexed—here was a most unusual case: two children clamouring for admittance into an establishment which every one else was averse to entering.

What was he to do with them? Were they to be left at the gates, to be sent back to Paroor? One thing was positively certain—they could not be received inside the jail.

A great multitude had now gathered to behold the convict's boy, who had walked seventy miles with his sister on his back. It takes but little at any time to attract an Indian audience. The crowd was about to be dispersed by the police, when the jail superintendent drove up in his brougham for his morning inspection, and alighted, and asked in amazement the reason of the tumult.

In five minutes he was in possession of all the facts—the thread of the story—much delayed by constant exclamations and additions from excited women in the throng.

"So these are thy children?" said the superintendent to Chūnnee.

"Yes, my lord; and it was for the sake of these that I tried to commit that theft."

"And thy brother hath turned them out?"

"So they say; and it was like him."

"Why hath he done so?"

"How can I tell thee, protector of the poor, save that he is a bad man? His name of Zālim Sing fits him but too well; truly he is a tyrannical lion. If the bountiful sirkar would only feed my children!"

"You cannot, of course, have these children with you; but I will look after them for you, at any rate, for the present. You shall see them again to-morrow. Here, burkundaz; send these children down to my house on an ekka, and let this crowd disperse."

As soon as the two objects of curiosity had been rattled off in charge of a warder, the assembly melted away, each to his own avocation.

The superintendent's wife was a charitable, gentle lady, and accepted the weary, half-starved wayfarers into her household. A servant—one of their own caste—shared his "go-down" with them, and they were bathed, fed, and their sores attended to. In a short time they looked totally different—such is the effect of kindness. They went to visit their father at stated periods, and when Girunda related his life of toil and blows at his uncle's hands, Chūnnee's straight brows grew very black.

The charitable lady who had given them a shelter did more than feed and clothe them; they were included among her servants' children, who learnt from a munshi, and were taught at her expense. The munshi, with his blue spectacles, sat in the midst of them, and every week there were prizes of fruit, and twice a year of clothes. They were also permitted to pick withered leaves in the lady's lovely garden, and Girunda was proud when he was allowed to carry a pot; and sometimes their father worked there also, with a few other favoured convicts. And oh, what a garden that was!—even to a *blasé* European eye, an exquisite spot; how much more to two ignorant native children, who have never seen any flowers but marigolds? The steps from the house led down into a great spreading lawn, green and smooth as velvet, and surrounded by wide walks, bordered with bushes of magnificent roses. Beyond the lawn, and leading straight out of it, lay an avenue of loquat trees, which was lined with stands of maiden-hair ferns, orchids, arum lilies, jheel plants—a truly fairy-like scene. There were long alleys overhung with fruit trees and flowers; there were enormous bushes of yellow roses—in one tree a pair of bulbuls had their nest—a large, square plot covered with a dense crop of variegated sweet peas. There was, moreover, a big vinery, a quantity of fruitful peach trees, a cote of pigeons, with nearly two hundred in the branches of a mango tree, and a house full of white rabbits with ruby eyes! Truly, when they were permitted to enter this garden, Girunda said to his sister, "Behold, this must be the place the preaching moola meant when he spoke of the garden of Paradise!"

The wheel of fortune turns, and strange events do occur at times, even in a mud village, in an obscure locality.

Old Turroo Sing had been wise in his generation; he had not grudged to offer a considerable reward for news of, or the recovery of, his lost treasure. For eight weary months no tidings reached him, and he had almost prepared to await the coming of death, a broken-hearted man, when, lo! one day six gay policemen—I allude to their red turbans, yellow trousers, and blue tunics—were once more seen approaching the village. The inspector had come to see Turroo, to confer with him privately. When the door was closed fast, the inspector drew forth a heavy gold bangle, and placed it in the old man's withered, trembling hands.

"Is this yours?" he asked.

"It is; it is; it is! Where are the rest?" clamoured Turroo.

"Patience! This was offered for sale in Delhi, and was about to be melted down. The man who sold it is in the village. He is Goora Dutt, the brother-in-law of thy nephew, Zālim Sing."

"May every curse light on him!" screamed the venerable Turroo.

"He was caught and convicted; he hath confessed. Thou wilt get nearly all thy property back, my father; but thou wilt be liberal to the police?"

"As I live, I will give much buchseesh, I swear it on the cow's tail!"

"There is a gang of gamblers here in Paroor. We have known it long. Goora Dutt is the chiefest among them. They were—for all things are known to the police—without money; they were in debt, and their creditors were hungry; therefore they agreed to rob thee, and they did. They carried off thy money and jewels.

Though Chūnnee Sing was convicted and sentenced for the same, he never fingered a tolah of gold nor one rupee."

"And where is it? where is it? Oh, speak!"

"It is buried by a neem tree near Goora Dutt's garden. They had no time to carry it farther, and it is convenient to their houses. The rupees are gone, but the gold and pearls and carbuncles are still mostly there. They feared to sell them, for the size and number and marks were known."

In half an hour's time Turroo Sing's treasure, which was buried in a kerosene-oil tin (oh, to how many uses are those tins put!), was dug up in the presence of the entire village, and shown to its owner, who wept with joy as he tore open the parcel and counted his pearls—his forty pairs without blemish. But there were some very glum faces in the crowd—four families were implicated in the robbery—and when Zālim Sing had come to overwhelm his grand-uncle with felicitations, that fierce old person had spat at him—like an infuriated toddy cat.

"Thou hadst a hand in it, oh, badmash, son of lies!" he screamed, foaming at the mouth. "Thy brother-in-law, Goora Dutt, is thy shadow. 'Twas he fetched the police for Chūnnee, who hath languished in jail for thy sins. Take this robber, and release Chūnnee Sing."

* * * * *

Zālim Sing's popularity had been on the wane for a considerable time. He had assured his neighbours in his most plausible manner, that Girunda and Gyannia had run away, ungrateful wretches that they were—just like their father, the jail-bird. But the neighbours believed a wholly different tale. A ryot, living in the nearest village, had met Zālim, one dark night, driving a pair of children before him. People began to whisper, and then to talk openly, of screams heard from Zālim's house; of the boy Girunda being seen carrying loads as heavy as a pony's—and now, after all these months, public opinion set in, in full tide, in favour of Chūnnee.

Zālim Sing had a presentiment that his good days were leaving him when he saw his friend Goora Dutt and four other men led away between the crops, with handcuffs on their wrists; and many a curious glance was cast at Zālim himself.

"How came his wife to wear a pearl nose-ring? How came he to possess *four* bullocks and a Waterbury watch and a pistol? Could any one give an honest reason? Could his crops have sold at double the rates of ours?" his neighbours asked one another. Truly, he was as great a thief as any; but his accomplices had been staunch to him, and had held their peace.

Of course Chūnnee was released, much to his own surprise. His ragged coat was restored to him one morning, with a "hookum," to say that he was free. His first duty was to return thanks to the benevolent lady who had rescued his starving children. He laid his head at her feet, and touched the hem of her gown; and there was a mist in his eyes as he said, "Now I understand why God suffered me to be put in the Jail Khana. It was that my children might know you. Eshwar, Eshwar will bless you always."

"And where will you go, Chūnnee?" she inquired, ere he took leave.

"Home," he answered: a native returns to his ancestral village as a Swiss turns to the mountains. "Back to Paroor and my house. It is true that I have no friends; but I have no friends anywhere. I was born there; also my father and grandfather. It is my country, and there will I die."

"It is more to the purpose, how will you live, once you are there?"

"I have good-conduct money. I shall hire a little bit of land, and dig it, and buy seeds. Girunda is growing big, he can help me."

He was not to be deterred by offers of employment in the city. No, his heart was set upon Paroor—only Paroor; and his kind patroness fitted out the children with clothes and food, and they bade farewell to her, and her enchanted garden, with many bitter tears.

Most of the journey was made by rail, and in the delightful novelty of the motion of a railway carriage they soon forgot their sorrows. The last twenty miles had to be accomplished on foot. Girunda stepped out manfully beside his father, who carried Gyannia. All *he* had to carry was the cat; and, moreover, he had now a pair of shoes and a stick.

They reached Paroor at nightfall, and Chūnnee went straight to his own hut. It was occupied by an old crone, who had bought it from Zālim Sing for six rupees, and who felt herself a proprietress of some importance. She thrust him out with a lighted brand, and Chūnnee and his family passed the night under a stack of straw.

The following morning he went and rapped boldly at his brother's door, and confronted him sternly.

"So thou art back, badmash! I wonder thou hast come here!" cried Zālim, with ill-simulated scorn.

"How daredst thou sell my house?" rejoined the other.

"I sold it to pay for thy children's food."

"Speak not of the children you worked as slaves, and beat, and turned out at night to perish. Restore the money and the house, O villain!"

Hearing loud and angry voices, the inevitable crowd collected. There was Chūnnee, looking quite well-to-do, and actually speaking in a commanding tone to his once all-powerful brother!

"Behold, he hath sold my poor hovel, and hath kept the money," explained Chūnnee, turning to the eager audience. "He hath beaten and starved my children, and hath thrust them out to die. Why do ye suffer such a sinner among you?"

The crowd began to clamour and howl, and Zālim Sing withdrew and barred his door; but the angry neighbours beat upon it till it shook on its rusty hinges, and Zālim Sing was forced to shout, "Go! thou shalt have thy house, O badmash." And for the first time in all his life, Chūnnee was beholden to the force of public opinion.

CHAPTER VI.

Old Turroo had heard of Chūnnee's arrival. Everything is known in a short time in a small community, save such matters as robbery and gambling, practised under the cover of darkness.

He sent for his grand-nephew—much to that grand-nephew's surprise—and beckoning him in with a long, claw-like finger, commanded him to close the door, and be seated on a charpoy. He then pushed his huka towards him, and coughed, and said—

"Thou art back, and I have much to say unto thee. How dost thou mean to live, and keep thy children, O Chūnnee Sing?"

"I hope to hire that plot of land near Ram Lall's garden, and till it by hand, and sow it with cotton, jawarri, and dál. I have recovered my house which Zālim Sing sold."

"Wouldst thou leave that dog-kennel, and come and abide here with me?"

"Here—with thee!" he echoed incredulously; he could not believe his ears.

"Yea. Hearken to me, Chūnnee, the son of Duloo Sing. It is in my mind to make thee mine heir. Thou hast suffered wrongfully for my treasure; it shall be thine one day."

"I did not take the money or jewels, it is true, O Turroo Sing, but it is true that I desired to steal them—not from love of lucre and gold, or the vice of robbery, but for the sake of my children, who were perishing. All that day the little ones tasted naught but cow's food. The boy asked thee for a few cowries, and thou gavest him blows; and an evil spirit tempted me as I walked in the fields at even, and said in mine ear, 'Turroo is rich—yea, very rich. He hath a house and land and cattle, and warm bedding, and brass cooking-pots, and a store of grain laid up in his granary for many seasons. Moreover, he hath a great treasure buried beneath his floor, which is of no profit to him, save to handle and to count. Behold, some of this useless silver will feed my children and me. I will dig through the wall, and steal, under the cover of darkness. The man is old; he sleeps fast. I shall take one hundred rupees, and be happy.' But I failed, as thou knowest. Nevertheless, I was guilty."

"Thou wert hungry, and thy children were crying for food; but Zālim Sing had no such excuse—he is a shaitan, the son of a she ass. Thou shalt take his place, and come after me; thou shalt live here now with thy children. Surely a strong man, with a lathi, is better than an aged chokedar and a dog! I may be robbed again; with thee I am safe; for doubtless thou wilt guard thine own. Let the old hag remain in thine hut, and bring thy children hither."

So, to the amazement of the village, Chūnnee, the pauper and the prisoner, was elevated to the right hand of the richest man in Paroor, and rose proportionately in every one's estimation. He tilled the land, and sold the crops, and cut the cane, whilst Girunda spent his time between the fields and the village munshi—as befitted a boy who would rise in the world, and perchance go to college!

His grand-uncle was proud of him, and never tired of boasting of Girunda's seventy-mile march with his sister on his back.

Gyannia now wears a gold nose-ring, silver bangles, and a chain—which gauds comprise most of her toilette. She is a happy infant, and passes her four sallow cousins in the narrowest lane, with her head in the air.

Her cousins and their father have resorted to every description of clever intrigue to get on terms with their lucky relatives, but in vain. It is the dream of Zālim Sing's life to bestow one of his sallow daughters in marriage on Girunda, and thus keep the fortune in the family; but it is not probable that the boy—who retains a lively recollection of the ladies' nips and blows and floutings—will ever meet his wishes. Moreover, Turroo has already a bride in view.

The cat prospers, though as lanky and grimy as of old; she must be a cat of some breeding, or of Chinese extraction, for when, after all her vicissitudes, she found herself once more in her native village, she did not exhibit the least surprise—she merely stretched out her long body, and strolled over and sharpened her claws in the bark of a familiar tree. She has accepted the transformation from poverty to wealth with complete equanimity, and sits washing her face outside Turroo's door, or surveys the village from the tree that grows through his roof, as if she had never lived elsewhere; she has also implanted a wholesome fear of her displeasure in the breast of Chondi the pariah. But then she is a cat who has travelled and seen the world, and he is but a common village cur!

Who would recognize Chūnnee Sing now? He wears a handsome turban, and coolies salaam to him, and address him as "ap." He rides on a white horse—yes, a horse, not a pony—with a long pink tail, and is the leading man in those parts; for all he takes in hand appears to thrive.

As he passes through the villages, coquettish glances from pretty dark eyes are cast at him, and he is greeted with playful remarks. Chūnnee is as much sought after now as he was formerly shunned. It is a matter of common talk that a rich thakur would gladly give him his daughter to wife; but Chūnnee appears satisfied with his present lot, and shows no signs of changing his condition.

Our story is ended, and we will now take leave of Chūnnee and his charger, of Gyannia and her ferret-faced cat, of Girunda—who is almost as precious to Turroo as the forty pairs of pearls again buried beneath the floor—of the envious, adder-tongued family of Zālim Sing—and cast a final glance on the sleepy patriarchal village, where it lies among its waving crops on the hillside, within sight of a glint of the sacred Ganges.

THE END.

9 789361 385926

Printed by Libri Plureos GmbH in Hamburg,
Germany